Shakespeare in South Florida

Christoph Paul

Caroline Macon Fleischer

Shakespeare in South Florida

Cover by Matthew Revert
ISBN: 9781960988652 (paperback)

CLASH Books
Troy, NY
clashbooks.com
Distributed by Consortium
First Edition 2026

To our inner teenagers
To our first loves
To our high school English teachers
To our prom dates
To Peaches

Act 1: Prologue

Our Hero Doth Protests Love & Indie Films

I was driving to see my shrink when I realized I, unfortunately, had everything figured out. The important stuff, anyway—like where I stood on the romantic spectrum as an aspiring filmmaker who hadn't touched a camera in seven years.

My epiphany driving to the shrink was this:

Women chose guys the same way people chose movies. Since I was a kid, all I'd wanted was to make films, but lately I watched them obsessively. I'd seen almost every movie ever made, which influenced my theory, but I was using science to prove its truth.

My biology teacher Mr. Wilkins had been teaching us about female choice. He was lame but smart, and he'd give me props on this theory since it matched Darwin's whole thing about hooking up and not dying.

I knew I was a seventeen-year-old virgin, but I was as street smart as a drug dealer. Sure, I was white—an Italian Jew or "Pizza Bagel," as they called me in seventh grade—and lived in suburban Delray Beach, but I had the smarts and I watched *The Wire*.

I should clarify: I wasn't an incel, but I did enjoy 4chan before I developed real taste.

In the hierarchy of who got hot girls, blockbusters sat at the top. Everyone loved seeing them. Even French kids and hipsters in fake glasses would see these movies because they were that good.

The guys in this category were tall and good-looking. They were awesome, impressive CGI eye candy that glued your eyes to the screen. They had high budgets and knew how to market themselves—they showed up and people wanted to see them. I hated admitting this because it showed life wasn't fair, but they were also entertaining: good plot, intelligent enough, fun to watch.

I was a movie snob who still enjoyed a good blockbuster. They might not be the deepest guys, but they had charismatic-huge-star appeal, which metaphorically meant they were dudes with well-sized penises. I'd say "good" but "well" was more grammatically correct and my English teacher Miss Connie kept bugging me about grammar.

Unfortunately for women, and fortunately for me, I'd noticed there weren't many of these guys around. Lately, lots of blockbusters sucked, and the good ones weren't free on Netflix. My parents had just switched from the Netflix DVD drop-off service to live-streaming, which meant the graveyard of unlimited monthly rentals without late fees in my drawer got cleaned out and replaced with something better (mechanical pencils without the lead, unlabeled USB drives, and Axe body spray). Anyway, I'd seen so many shitty blockbusters the last couple years.

Sigh. Men and movies.

These guys were oafing around locker rooms,

cracking Chuck Norris jokes, shopping at Abercrombie. They could go out with any girl they liked, except maybe the goths. Even still, I heard those chain-wearing, Hello Kitty-loving girls who smoked under the bleachers were hot-tubbing with the football team on inconspicuous weeknights. These people couldn't wait to get the keys to their first Mazda Miata. All flash that fizzled—eye candy wrapped in exhaust and noise.

To be fair, they did have really cool cars.

Below shitty blockbusters came romantic comedies. First, the favorites—tried and true. You knew these films. Think of your top five rom-coms. These were good ones that almost everyone loved. Even the hardest cynics secretly enjoyed them. As men, these were guys who were likable and funny. I really wished I was one of these guys. They had good social skills, could make jokes that were funny without making people uncomfortable, were good at connecting and sharing feelings, had above-average looks, or were chubby guys who were still hot, like Seth Rogen.

But there were way more bad rom-coms than good ones. In those, the dudes were straight-up lame, corporate guys presented as quirky but misunderstood. They weren't misunderstood. They existed to be annotated and verbally battered by women who liked a challenge. Meh. I was sure those chicks got bored and moved to Brooklyn or something once the pop-song credits were done rolling.

Below those types came the horror and thriller movies. These were psycho guys who could be thrilling because they were challenging or fucked up in a fun way. I was screwed up, but not in an interesting or sexy way like Ghostface. What was it with teenage girls learning how to masturbate after watching *Scream*?

Thrillers were thrilling at first, but after a few bad dates redeemed by what I assumed was good sex, it got annoying to feel nervous they'd go postal or fight someone at the mall. These types of guys weren't family-friendly, either. After a while, women felt like these dudes were sequels they were sick of seeing. They'd get bored and go meet a sensible man at church.

Even below that, at the bottom of everything, stood my ranking: The Indie Art Film.

Indie art film guys like me were average-looking, average height, average penis. No big star power. No special effects. My budget sucked—I'd never even had a job.

I'd been told I was strange, and not in the good way goth or hipster girls were into. I was strange in that bogus DVD-section-at-the-library type of way because I had no real niche and seemed to pass through society like an unaddressed dust bunny.

I had bland brown hair, and no matter how hard I tried, I could never get a cool haircut because it was so frizzy and curly. My life would've been better if I had cool hair. I sucked at sports and had—quote-unquote—issues, which was always the plot of indie art films. It was hard for me to connect with most people and make friends. I was the kid picking dandelions behind the baseball field before the coach not-so-kindly suggested I "switch to drama or something." I did do that, but I'll get to that later, and screw him anyway. My journey had nothing to do with his stupid suggestion. In any case, my school was so pathetic you wouldn't believe it was real.

But back to my awakening regarding film genres as romantic prospects.

Indie art films were sometimes depressing. We

didn't always have happy endings, and we were tough to figure out, or maybe too easy to figure out. We didn't always make sense, and sometimes we were stupid and self-absorbed. Should I be like a French one and get all depressed? Sure. I was already depressed so why not get myself a black turtleneck? I'd burn less whenever my parents dragged me to Atlantic Dunes Park.

Every other day I'd say I was screwed and ask my shrink to up my Effexor, but there was one good thing about being the indie art film: everyone had one little quirky one they truly loved. A film had a major, lasting impact on their life. The one they'd own and never sell or lose. The one they'd shell out for the Criterion edition with all the extras.

The hardest part was finding that one person who dug me as a whole movie. But peeling off I-95 toward my shrink's office in Boca Raton, I felt like maybe I'd found her.

That 'her' was Alexia Marcos.

Act 1: Scene 2

In Banana Pudding, Hereth a Meetcute

The same road held the magical place where I first met Alexia. Not at therapy, but at an even less sexy place—my grandma's retirement home, conveniently located near my shrink.

I visited Grandma's retirement home three times a week and volunteered to run their Bingo game. I had to do this or get a real job.

It was dinner time when I went to get pudding for Grandma. The Beach Boys were playing because old Boomers were obsessed with them. I grabbed her favorite organic FAGE banana pudding when I heard a sweet Cuban surfer-girl voice say, "Hey, can you help me bring the pudding to the table?"

I turned around as the "God Only Knows" chorus played, and saw a curly-haired brunette with big green eyes and a shy sweet smile. And a body like a Coke bottle, like the 00s rap songs talked about. And her voice matched that sweet vanilla acidity—warm and a little smoky.

Mine didn't. "Ugh. Um? Oof. Sure."

I picked up the extra tray and followed the mystery volunteer to the dining area. It resembled an upscale middle school cafeteria where boys sat with boys and girls sat with girls unless they were coupled up. Yeah. That social structure remains true even amongst widows and divorcées.

Mr. Klein and his crew were the bad boys of the retirement home. They were debating the Miami Dolphins' new quarterback, but one had fallen asleep with his head on the table. When the beautiful brunette approached, they all became speechless.

"You guys want some pudding?" she asked.

"Victor, wake up! You gotta see this shiksa," Mr. Klein yelled, shaking his friend awake so hard the guy let out a fart that filled the whole cafeteria. The sound was so loud it knocked Alexia off-balance, falling back into me. We fell to the ground along with the pudding cups while the fart ricocheted off spoons and mixed with The Beach Boys' final chorus.

Woah. I hadn't been this close to a girl since ever.

Infinity passed, and we started laughing along with the old men at Mr. Klein's table. We should have gotten up, but we just lay there while the old people began arguing about manners and courtesy and where the janitor was. The girl and I kept laughing, belly laughs getting stronger as we sludged and squeaked, shoving aside mounds of plastic and the goop of exploded pudding. I found a half-soaked napkin somewhere in the pile and wiped bits of the sweet goo off my mouth, feeling it stinging my eyes, and finally the laughter slowed. Alexia wiped her hands on her back pocket. She widened her eyes and gave a dramatic sigh.

"Yikes. Hey." I caught my breath. "I'm Joseph. My friends and non-friends call me Caldo." She kept smiling but didn't say anything. "Not that you're not my friend. Or you could be my friend. Once I know you. Because that's how friendships happen." I coughed. "Caldo is my last name."

"Alexia. Cool to meet you, Caldo."

We shook hands while still on the ground. "Sorry. I'll clean this up."

"We can do it together."

I got up first, then reached down to help her up, amazed at myself for acting so gracefully when I felt like a puny little frog. She wanted to help me? What the fuck? How was I not blowing this? Her hand felt good—it fit right in mine.

We went to the napkin station in the corner, and my curiosity came out. "I gotta say it. You don't seem Jewish. Or old. What are you doing here at the Rothstein Retirement Home?"

"Yeah, I'm Cuban and a little bit French."

She looked embarrassed, but it was anyone's guess why, since she was so cute. I waited for her to elaborate, but she wasn't giving any clues, so I pushed further. "We survived a fart assault. I think honesty is the only policy at this point."

I'd never made a girl laugh before, not in a nice way, but apparently she thought I was a riot. She shrugged in a way that was somehow both endearing and hot.

"I'm here because I'm court-ordered." Then, she leaned closer and lowered her voice. "But keep quiet. I'm not proud of it."

Not proud of it? To be an adorable criminal? She was a femme fatale. I was the luckiest guy in the world, imagining picking her up from jail in leather on a motorcycle. "Hey, I don't judge. Mom's Jewish, so I'm basically court-ordered here to visit Grandma."

Another laugh! The embarrassed look on her face returned to her normal chill-I'm-hot-but-I-don't-think-of-myself-as-that-hot expression. I didn't know what my face was doing. Probably looking like a goof because I was falling in love in real time.

"It's nice to have another young person here."

"You're telling me."

Cleaning the pudding off the floor took forever. I just wanted to talk more.

But alas, Grandma demanded I come back over. I slunk over, the wind out of my sails, and tuned out the table of old ladies as they problematically discussed Alexia's "unusual" and "striking" olive skin.

For the next hour, I watched her like a hopeful puppy, desperate to catch her attention. We met eyes three whole times—I wished it had been four—then finally dinner ended. She was hard to read but seemed intrigued. Once she finished tossing dishes into the bus bin, she initiated direct contact. She tipped her head toward the exit and mouthed, "Wanna hang outside?" I didn't bother to say goodbye to Grandma and her friends. They'd give me a hard time later, but it would be worth it.

I followed her out of the dining hall, which developed a raucous Denny's energy whenever the sun set. I followed behind her through the heavily air-conditioned lobby, at last through the doors into the ultimate teen-boy rite of passage: standing outside in iconic South Florida heat with a pretty girl.

She pulled out a hot pink Zippo and lit a Marlboro Light with impressive muscle memory. Mom made me too paranoid to ever try cigarettes, but damn, despite all the horrible cancer statistics wheeling around in my head, Alexia looked sexy as hell smoking.

"Want one?"

"Nah, the D.A.R.E. assemblies got to me."

She rolled her eyes and grinned. "Those are so lame."

"So is smoking," I said too fast. "I mean, in the opinion of those who don't smoke. I don't judge."

"I need at least two vices."

"What's your other vice?"

"It was drinking, but after the DUI and getting sent to AA, it's binge-watching television."

Vulnerability shone through her brown eyes, so I tried to mirror it.

"I am kind of lame. I don't drink or smoke." Then, I felt like I needed to toughen up, so I crossed my arms and added, "But I am on meds." My bullshit cracked her up again, so I kept the open mic going. "I'm obsessed with television, too. Mostly movies. But it's hard to say anything is bad. Everything was made for a reason—there's something for everyone."

"I know what you mean. I'm on meds, too. They do help. Not partying is for the best, but it's hard to feel cool anymore."

"You look cool. Too cool for school."

"Nah. I'm a freshman at FAU. I feel like I don't fit in, and it sucks. People only connect with one another when they're fucked up."

"I don't think that's true."

"No?"

"We're bonding over banana pudding. And farts."

She switched her cigarette to the other hand so she could chew on her thumbnail. A smokestack with a nervous habit. God, help me. And we both seemed to be struggling with our own bullshit. "Can you hold this for a second?" she asked, handing me the cigarette. I took it and she put her hand under her armpit and made a chicken wing fart.

"See? It could be worse. I'm still a senior. I'm going to a weird one-on-one tutoring school to finish high school. It's like a revamped H&R Block with grade schoolers on the other side. Super depressing place, and all the students on my side are the worst. They're fucking crazy. Listen to this shit: I'm like the most normal person there. If you can even imagine."

"Wow." Her eyes expanded wide like two big balloons. "You know a place is bad when you're the sanest person there." She sucked air through her teeth. "That sounds like the worst."

"Totally the worst. A bunch of screwed-up kids that belong in juvie or a mental hospital, not a learning establishment. I don't hang out with any of them, so I visit Grandma. I don't want to brag, but calling Bingo is my social life."

My honesty shocked me. Usually, I was slow to open up. She had a way with me.

"Damn, you do get around. What meds are you on? I'm on Paxil and Lithium."

"Adderall and Effexor. ADHD and depression aren't as hardcore as alcoholism and manic depression, but I know the struggle," I held out my fist, and she pounded it playfully.

"Jesus. We are some fucked-up Floridians." She took another drag.

"So do you believe Jesus is the Messiah?"

"Ha!"

I felt so excited and wigged out, sharing a moment of intimacy. I eagerly went for another subject, like a quiz to see how much we had in common. "Do you watch *The Wire*?"

"God. Why are white guys in Palm Beach County obsessed with *The Wire*?"

"Hey now! No. It's the only show that's better than a movie."

"Riiiiight."

"It's like. It's art."

"I'm one to talk. I'm obsessed with *Gilmore Girls*." She leaned back and squinted her eyes, looking me up and down, analyzing me. "You are such a Jess."

I rolled my eyes playfully. "Please don't make me Google what that means. So, Miss Gilmore Girl, how long do you have to volunteer here?" I hoped it would be at least five years.

"Five hundred hours. We'll see each other more. If I come three days a week, it should only take ninety days." She paused and teetered her weight back and forth.

"You look like you want to ask me something."

She cocked her head to the side. "No, it's fine."

"What?" I shrugged. "We both admitted we have mental illness and have no friends. Go ahead."

"Is there any chance you can give me a ride here? I lost my license, and the bus system sucks."

I screamed internally but had to play it chill. "Sure," I said, forcing casualness. I went to pop my collar but I didn't have one, so I scratched my neck instead. "I visit Grandma Goldstein on Mondays, Wednesdays, and Fridays. At least until I get a job. I can give you a ride after school."

"It's a date! My hero."

I cheesed out at the word date and prayed this would be the start of my film. Ideally, I'd be the hunky Bradley Cooper type, but I could settle for some tormented stud like Mark Ruffalo.

Maybe I'd call it *Caldo: A Hero's Journey*, but with my luck, I'd get stuck in the role of a Shakespearean fool like in those plays Miss Connie made us read. My destiny was an inevitable tragedy. Yep—that would be it. Viewers would feel the secondhand embarrassment of a meta film to be forgotten while I clowned my way into my own grave. I was fucked. This would only end in heartbreak.

Act 1: Scene 3

To Coitus One's Way from Sorrow

Pretend you pressed fast forward to eighty-something days later.

While fast forwarding, you'd see Alexia and me driving together. Business as usual in our new, synchronized routine. A typical Wednesday afternoon.

Only not. Me being head-over-high-top-Converse in love.

We'd graduated to that picturesque next level: legs touching, her telling me I was cute. It built up until boom—Alexia and I were cruising past palm trees in my creaking Honda Accord when she put in a mix CD that opened with Peaches' "Fuck the Pain Away."

It was like in episode three of *The Wire,* when everyone is minding their business then suddenly Omar and his henchman show up and steal everybody's narcotics. Peaches was my Omar. My innocence was the narcotics. Peaches, that wicked electropunk Canadian, robbed me of the relative homeostasis of life before love.

Alexia sang along like she was reciting nonchalant bad-girl poetry.

> *Sucking on my titties*
> *like you haunting me,*
> *balling me,*
> *all of the wine*

Wow. I didn't know the lyrics, but I knew those were not them. Either way, one day I was a kid on a tricycle and the next, there was a woman saying the word "titties" in my presence. Body parts that she herself had. In the car with me. She looked at me and danced in the passenger seat, goofy in her way.

> *What else is in*
> *the freak list of Peaches?*
> *Huh? Butt?*

I didn't know what to say. I didn't know what else was in the freak list of Peaches. How confused I was that I hoped the curriculum would teach me how to bang somebody properly and maybe even make love to them. Love? What was wrong with me—I should've wanted to mimic porn, then worry about that crap later. But this wasn't porn. It was a whole other genre. Something softer. And damn, that song captured a rugged but sensual vibe.

My AC was broken that week, but it was spot-on for the moment. Our sweaty thighs stuck to our chairs, the seatbelts hot on our skin. Alexia smelled like chlorine and Banana Boat, a bikini still wet underneath her clothes after a day at the pool. Water marks on her so-called titties. Swimming and baking in the sun with a book, all while I'd been rotting in my goosebumps at school. She rolled her hand in waves in the warm breeze out the window. When we started the driving arrangement, I'd asked her not to smoke in my car and she respected that—but at that moment, I wanted to tell her to go for it anyway. I couldn't. My mom would murder me. Alexia kept singing the horny chorus.

The teachings of Peaches included a promise to end all suffering. I was sold.

Then we gave each other the look—the one I'd only seen in theaters and dreams. That catchy-ass chorus gave me the courage to say what had been on my heart in a more direct way.

"Hey, Alexia?"

"Hey, Caldo?"

"I want to, um—I'm sorry. I want to—fuck the pain away. Uh? That was a joke. I want to call you all the time. I'm kidding." Oh no. I was earning an F in direct communication. She smirked. I smiled. "I'm sorry. I want to—what I mean is—I wanna go on a date with you. Like a Peaches date. I mean, not a fucking date. But, um, romantic. In nature. Would that be okay?"

"Sure, why not? YOLO."

"Does that mean yes?" I asked, scared, because a pop culture reference wasn't a definitive yes or no.

"Yeah. I like spending time together. Let's have some fun and see what's here."

"Like, dinner?"

"That sounds good. Then we can go back to my dorm room, and I'll give you your premiere VIP screening of *Gilmore Girls*."

Be still my heart.

"It's a date." Saying it out loud cemented it as truth. "YOLO it is!"

Act 1: Scene 4

Our Hero Endures Coach and Counsel

As a newly minted potential suitor, my Thursday afternoon appointment with my shrink, the ole Dr. Heller, came at the perfect time. I pulled into the parking lot still in disbelief about what was going to happen on Friday: my date with Alexia. Unless I died before then, and it's fucked up that's where my mind goes, but there we were.

I admit, though, the combination of cool-guy energy and fraught anxiety made me feel complicated and interesting. Seeing myself in the rearview mirror, the scrunch of worry forever plastered into my eyebrows had transformed from looking like I'd shat myself to being compelling and intriguing to the female sort. On top of that, the hot, shaded parking garage that had felt mundane for months now worked like a Hollywood set piece. The dim light made me feel like the leading man of a moody, sexy teen movie. Nerves and swagger in my step. I slipped my sunglasses to the top of my shaggy head.

But I zoomed out and saw myself, incapable of fully

enjoying these moments of fantasy because of this event seven years ago that made me hate myself. The event that put me in therapy in the first place. When I was younger and obsessed with making films, I filmed everything I saw. In our old neighborhood, there was this old guy who would walk around talking to himself. He was on Bluetooth, but I was a kid—I didn't know. All I knew was I had to film him. Even though I wasn't behind the camera anymore, I still viewed the world this way. All of life's stuff became more significant onscreen.

I started following him after my parents got me a camera for Chrismukkah. Following him felt like a necessary, unexplained instinct. One day, he noticed I was following him and lost his shit, cursing at me and telling me to get lost.

But the art came first. The more he acted up, the more I wanted to keep filming him.

He called me a commie spy and ran for his life. It was cinematic gold—me chasing after him and catching all the paranoid things he had to say. But then art lost control of reality. Up ahead, I saw a car backing up fast out of a driveway. I screamed at the old man to watch out, but he ran straight into the car. I saw the situation so clearly then: I was a kid with a stupid dream, and he paid the price for it. The collision broke six of his bones. His family didn't sue, but my parents had to pay the hospital bills. Selling my camera was how my parents paid for some of it, and Mom refused to get me a camera ever again. Cinema wasn't the same when it was captured on some dumb phone.

That day felt like a million years ago, but it had only been seven. The worst punishment should have been the cost to my parents, their disappointment, the innocent man's injuries, or even my guilt. But instead, it was losing access to my favorite thing—my video camera.

There I was, feeling suddenly uncool. The sexy teen movie had dissipated, and I was a pathetic kid sitting in the waiting room of my shrink's office, knowing that everything about life had gotten worse since that day.

"Joseph. Good to see you. How's school going?" Reba the secretary asked. She made everyone feel better, almost even better than the shrink himself.

"It's going. My English teacher Miss Connie is having me do stuff with the grade school kids about Shakespeare. On the high school side, all the kids are still crazy, but I'm here, so I can't throw stones. How are things going with your son? Isn't he going for an MBA? Those guys are always villains in the movies, but they score the best chicks."

"I am proud of him, Joseph, and he's happy. But math and business aren't everything. Reading Shakespeare in college truly helped me find myself and what makes me happy. You'll find that too. It's good to hear you are working with kids. Working with kids will make you more mature."

She handed me the sign-in clipboard and a lime green curly pen that'd likely been ransacked from a goodie bag. "Mature like this?" I asked, holding up the pen.

"I have some Dum-Dums, too. Be sure to grab one before you go."

Then, the door to the offices opened, interrupting our Mr. Rogers moment. The solemn Dr. Heller. "Hi, Joseph. Come on in."

I followed him into his office—a stereotypical setting: nice couch, big brown desk, a chair that looked like it belonged to Zeus up on Mount Olympus towering over the measly mortal's couch, many impressive degrees I didn't know how to interpret, and a bookcase with books about Freud and other dead white dudes who were smarter than me and even Dr. Heller himself.

Heller was a semi-normal dude—like Hannibal Lecter, but vegetarian and with a dad bod. I just came out with it. "I really like Alexia. Like romantically."

Dr. Heller chuckled. "We are getting right to it, aren't we? Though I must say, after you talked about how hot she was for at least ten minutes every session we've had, this isn't a surprise. You've never believed there was a romantic possibility?"

"Well, I've done the work, and I've come up with this theory that I have a shot at being her boyfriend and losing my virginity to her."

"Let's back up for a sec here, Joseph. You're putting a lot of eggs in the Alexia basket."

"You mean like if she is ovulating?"

"No." Dr. Heller swallowed back a laugh. He was permanently committed to the bit of seriousness. "What I mean is you have developed serious feelings for her. She is also something extra rare—a friend, which has been very tough to come by for you—and now there's a possibility of a romantic involvement."

"We can't be friends if I get boners when she's around. But you're right. It is more than that, though she does kinda look like this one chick whose performances I enjoy on Brazzers."

"Joseph, I'm barely on Facebook."

"In any case, from an acting and production standpoint, those films are very well done. You'd think it'd all be big boobs and hollow plots, but some of these writers are really onto something. Probing at the human psyche. Anyway, I don't watch it that much. I checked it out, like, a few times. Twenty tops. Look, I'm a romantic man, but you know, sometimes I can't picture girls in my head. But Alexia—she is better than porn. But as I explained, I don't watch porn for the women, anyway."

"I see."

"Alexia laughs at my jokes, too. She compliments me and stuff. Like she can really see me. Me! I know. She even said I was cute like four and a half times."

"Where does your theory come in?"

"I feel like she's the one girl who could actually get me and appreciate me."

"There are many girls in the world who I'm sure would appreciate you, Joseph."

"Pfft. Was that a joke? You make jokes now?"

"No."

"Okayyy-yuh." I picked up a fidget spinner he'd left on the side table as a tinker toy and got to work, trying to dispel the heavy feeling. I shifted. He didn't. I wondered how many people went in there and didn't know what to say. The teachings of Dr. Heller would be a song about patience and getting comfortable with awkward silences. He didn't break eye contact. I did. Twice.

"Take a breath."

But I jumped straight into blabbing again. "I'm going to take her to IHOP tomorrow after we leave my grandma's retirement home. Then we are gonna watch *Gilmore Girls*."

"*Gilmore Girls*. It's a date-date."

"Don't give me that. It's a show to be taken seriously. She would know."

"I can appreciate that. I watched it with my wife."

"Is it good?"

"It's really a perfect show."

I scratched my chin. Had Dr. Heller been a baller this whole time, or did I just now notice it? I tested my luck. "So you're a P.I.M.P."

He passively blew his nose and threw the tissue in the can under his seat. "What are your hopes for the evening? What would make a successful date?"

"Not totally bombing. Maybe like second base."

"You're hoping for physical affection. Are you going to try to kiss her? If the moment presents itself?"

"I hope so."

"And maybe more?"

"I don't know. I think it would change me. I want to know what that change would feel like."

"I'm not able to explain that to you, Joseph, but whatever happens, I will be here to listen and support you."

After the session, I drove home and found Dad watching sitcoms while Mom made dinner. The familiar sounds of domestic life—the laugh tracks, the sizzling garlic and onions from the kitchen, Mom occasionally screaming to ask why things kept disappearing from the fridge—felt comforting after spilling my guts to Dr. Heller.

"So what, the ranch got up and walked out on its own?" she asked. A few moments later, I guess no one responded fast enough. "Forget it. We'll eat our salad dry."

A commercial came on. My dad muted the TV. "How was your appointment?"

"Good. I think tomorrow's gonna be big."

Dad couldn't answer before Mom charged out from the kitchen, wiping her hands on a dish towel. "I miss everything. What's tomorrow night?"

"My date with Alexia."

"The college girl from the nursing home?" Her eyebrows shot up. "Joseph, she's too old for you. And she's not even Jewish."

"She's eighteen, Mom. And she's really cool."

"Cool doesn't pay the bills," Mom said. "You need to focus on your grades and getting into a good college. Maybe computer science—those boys make good money."

Dad tried to save me. "Let the kid have his date, Dawne. He's seventeen."

"Exactly! He's seventeen and thinking with his groin instead of his noggin."

I stood up, feeling suddenly protective of whatever was happening between Alexia and me. "My groin, Mom? You don't even know her."

"I know she's court-ordered to be at a nursing home," Mom shot back. "That tells me everything I need to know."

"She made a mistake. People make mistakes."

"Not under my watch! Find a nice Jewish girl!" Then, she softened slightly. "I'm sorry, Joey. I don't want you to get hurt."

"I won't." But I wasn't sure I believed it myself.

"Just be careful, son. And be home by midnight."

"It's not even a school night."

"Midnight. You'll call if you're going to be late. But you won't be late. Let me repeat. You. Will. Not. Be. Late."

Whenever she hacked her speech to pieces like that,

I knew she wasn't playing. "Yes, ma'am." I headed upstairs to pretend to do homework. My stomach churned with terror and glee. I dragged a blue-collared shirt and some khakis out of my drawer and threw them in the dryer with a scented sheet so they wouldn't wrinkle or stink. I rummaged through the underwear bin, through pairs of boxers with Teenage Mutant Ninja Turtles, American flags, and SpongeBob's square pants printed on them. Finally, a plain black pair and two matching white socks. I scrubbed the sides of my Converse with a Windex wipe until my hands were pruned.

Tomorrow night would change everything—I could feel it.

Act 1: Scene 5

A Most Lamentable School Day

Friday at last.

I wore some usual wrinkled scum, but laid my date clothes down flat in the trunk for later. The school day dragged on and on until it was lunchtime. For lunch, I always hung out in my car to avoid dealing with the loony kids on the one-on-one high school side, but parents complained. It did look pretty creepy for a young adult male to chill in his car while kids played on a playground. I considered buying an "I Hate Sex Offenders" bumper sticker to ward them off, but decided to eat lunch in my room instead.

Miss Connie was sitting by the window with book-patterned curtains she'd sewn at home herself. She had one hand around a chicken salad wrap and another weighing down the page of some big-ass edition of Shakespeare's classics. "Mr. Caldo, nice of you to join me. I got sick of staring at a wall during lunch and decided to bring my own reading material."

"I'm sorry, Miss Connie. Most guys would avoid

eating lunch with their teacher, but I decided to be a better man."

She licked some potato chip dust off her finger and handed me a Dr. Pepper from her mini fridge. I pulled a can of peas out of my backpack and dumped it into a Tupperware of cold rice. Ever since my mom quit packing my lunches, I did what I could to survive.

I nodded at her book. "I was talking to a grad student who works at the gas station about Shakespeare. He works there during the day to finish a Master of English degree at night."

"He sounds very cultured."

"Right. It's a really inspiring story. It motivates me to intellectualize."

"I can't tell if you're being sardonic."

"I'm always sincere. I just come across as sardonic. That's, like, the whole problem."

"I'd say I don't suffer fools gladly, but you wouldn't get the reference. Here's a reference you'll get—you're late all the time. I like having you here, Caldo. But three strikes? You're out. Since you were late yesterday, your penance is to read Shakespeare to the first graders for half of your lunch period. I selected *A Midsummer Night's Dream* for you."

I groaned. "They're like ten. Can't we make sock puppets or something?"

"You can ask your high-brow friend from the gas station to help you. They are hardworking and gifted children who—unlike you, no offense—do not need to be cajoled to appreciate great literature. I know you love movies, Mr. Caldo, but your dramatic writing adaptation assignment was a flop. There would be no movies if it weren't for literature, especially Shakespeare. Can you try to engage more? Please?"

"I'm sorry." I'd felt blocked from moviemaking since I put that old guy in the hospital. "As of now, I'm off the market for a screenwriting career. But hey, I want to learn more about the Shakespeare stuff."

"Did I hear that right?"

"Maybe that fiction stuff can help me learn about real-life stuff."

"Shakespeare? And please stop referring to him and everything else as 'stuff.'"

"Yeah, Shakespeare. My gas station homie said it can be useful with girls."

She huffed. "So literature is only good when it can maybe help you get girls?"

"Eh." I made a more-or-less hand gesture. I'd been caught, but clarified. "But hey. I totally paid attention in class when Mr. Wilkins talked about female choice in biology. So my thing is I've been courting a girl, old school style, like when you dated in the fifties or whatever, but I think I need to go even more old school and write her a sonnet or something to have a real shot to be her beloved or whatever."

"I dated in the seventies. It was very different from the fifties." A little smile snuck out. "Who is this special girl?"

"Alexia. She's a college girl who volunteers at Grandma's nursing home."

"By choice or court-ordered?"

"Why does everyone keep asking me that?"

Her smile faded.

"Look, she's got her issues, just like me and the kids who go here, but she's a good person. It's not just because she's super hot. It's like her heart is super hot too."

"How poetic." She said with a desert-dry tone.

"Well, Joseph, we will read more of Shakespeare's comedies, and you will learn a lot about love through them."

"Hell yeah."

"Don't get too excited. Shakespeare also wrote some plays where love leads to unbearable tragedy." She went back to her chicken salad and muttered, "I can see where this is going." She threw out her lunch and left the room for a meeting.

God. What did she know? I checked my phone. No texts or messages from Alexia that she was sick or needed to cancel. AKA things were going great.

Act 1: Scene 6

Wherein Every Hero Hath Fools and Jesters

Connie was gone and so was our food. I looked through the little window and spotted someone approaching. I knew it was Jamie because she always came to my room at this exact time. She knocked five times to ask her five questions. The principal said to humor her, but whatever—she had OCD or something. Everyone at that school had something.

Jamie was at least nice—not like the others. Actually, that wasn't true; there was Michelle, who had nonverbal autism. She stayed in her room and solved puzzles. Sometimes I'd come in and talk about life or my lack of it. She seemed to like the company and would look up not when I said anything interesting, but when she figured out a tough puzzle piece.

The five knocks came, and I heard Jamie behind the door. "Are you mad at me, Joey? Do you think the world is coming to an end? Are you eating a cheese sandwich today? Do you think Fane is planning on attacking me today? Do you think it's going to rain today?"

I was about to give my daily list of no's, but I wasn't

sure about the weather, so that one thwarted me. Then, in walked Fane, her hair faded from cerulean to Kool-Aid backwash. She was wearing a shirt with a picture of a skeleton cutting its arm bone open with a razor blade. She cracked a tiny bubble of old, hard gum then spat it into her palm and placed it on the windowsill. "Doesn't matter what Caldo says. I have leeches in my backpack. I'm going to put them in your tampons."

Yes. Somehow, there was a bully at a one-on-one tutoring school, and Fane was that bully.

"No. NO," Jamie screamed. "Please stop doing weird things to my tampons!"

"It's already done," Fane said, flashing her socio-pathic smile.

"I gotta go to CVS again," Jamie said. "You never think about the consequences." She charged out of the room, slamming the door behind her. No one really reacted. It was a normal interaction between Fane and Jamie. Fane messed with all of us, but she enjoyed picking on Jamie the most. Fane was androgynous and lost-seeming in general, so her being the bully of the school was a twisted sort of progress. At least it gave her some agency.

"I'm leaving! I'm going to talk to Michelle. It's nice that she doesn't talk back."

Jamie left to see her, our non-verbal autistic student, Michelle. She was sixteen and didn't seem to mind hearing the crazy things that came out of our mouths. She was honestly the only person I semi-liked at the school.

"God. Jamie is easy to torture relentlessly. I'm going to preserve one of those tampons in a jar as a memento," Fane said. She whipped a laptop out of her backpack and plugged it in. "Give me a sec before I start announcements. I'm hitting this girl up on OKCupid, and she looks like a goth Kristen Bell. I should message her that." Ever since Fane turned eighteen a month ago, all she did was bully people and rewrite her whole personality on her OKCupid profile. After typing for a minute, she shoved her laptop to the side. "Thank you for your patience."

"What's on the agenda?" I asked flatly. Fane pretended she had some sort of formal role in telling us all what to do. The best thing, I learned, was to go with it to save myself the headache of getting chewed out for no reason. It was nice not to be bullied, cause when I was at public school, this guy named Tony Rizzio made my life a living hell. He truly enjoyed making me feel bad and I get that same energy from Fane. Last I heard, Rizzio was making a name for himself as a SoundCloud rapper—psychopaths either struggle in the SoundCloud or succeed in the boardroom.

"I got news to share with whoever here is least likely to be in special ed."

"We all should be in special ed, you included," I said. "What news is so important?"

"We have a new girl coming. I saw Mrs. Judy give this super dorky but kinda hot Latina girl a tour. She's gonna start next week."

"What do you mean, dorky?"

"What, are you already sizing her up before you even meet her?"

I scratched my head, annoyed. "What the fuck else do you want me to do after an intro like that?

"Look, I get it, Caldo. I'm on your side. I'm a lesbian right now. Here's the profile: she has glasses and wears lame clothes to hide her figure like she's J-Lo pretending to be Amish. I couldn't tell if she had an ass, but she walked like she had a can of potpourri stuck up it. At the very least, she keeps baby wipes by the toilet. Clean cut. A toothbrush-in-her-backpack type. Probably still uses a Walkman. A lanyard-type girlie. Definitely straight, but that never stopped me at my last boarding school. Even back before I decided to go full-on butch—I'm still not entirely sold on that, but no matter. Hell, with you and Señor Dildo being the only guys around, she'll at least be bi-curious after her first week here. She's absolutely corruptible." She crossed her arms. "And don't get any ideas because it's my responsibility first."

Side note: Señor Dildo was the only other guy at my school. He was a fifteen-year-old little toad named Charles. His second day here, he hit on Fane, and she spat on his crotch in a pointedly non-sexual way and called him a Dildo. He took that as a sexual advance and got suspended for bringing her a gift-wrapped dildo in return. The kid even included a nice Hallmark card and a Chipotle burrito that was still hot.

Yes, this was my reality. Yet somehow Mom thought this place was better for me than public school.

I tried to picture this hot, dorky Amish-dressing Latina, but all my mind could see was the brown hair and green eyes of Alexia. "She's all yours. I have a date tonight."

"Yeah, right. Prove it."

"No."

"Then how will you know if you have a real shot?"

"Fine. Give me your laptop. Fane still had her Facebook open, so I searched up Alexia and revealed her profile picture. She was caked in glitter, eating whipped cream from the can.

"Are you kidding?"

"She got sober since then."

"That's not what I mean. I mean, are you serious? There's no chance she's into you."

That stung. I gave the laptop back. "Look. I know I'm not super hot or whatever. But don't, like, connections matter?"

"Maybe to divorcées with three kids."

I hated when Fane got under my skin. She was ruining my life hours before the big night. "Well, Fane, then why did she agree to go on a date with me? Huh?" I shot back. "We're watching *Gilmore Girls* for chrissake."

She tisked with skepticism, then pity. "Caldo, she watches *Gilmore Girls*. She's a sorority sister in disguise—girls like that aren't going to go for you. Nope. Also, she's got that crazy girl vibe. Is she medicated or what?"

"She does have some issues, yes."

"Well, that's good. Huh." She tapped her chin. "If she has mental disabilities and psychological weaknesses, maybe you could tap that."

"Wow, Fane. You might be the only genderqueer misogynist in the entire fucking world."

She glared at me. "I'm an individual. I read Nietzsche."

"He was a misogynist, too!"

"Okay, Psych 101. I don't need your slave morality."

My cheeks were hot. "I don't want to take advantage of anyone. I want her to like me for me." I crossed my arms, cementing how profound I was.

Then, Charles dropped in. AKA Señor Dildo. "No girl is going to do that, Caldo," he said. "You're destined for the friendzone." Fane showed him Alexia's Facebook picture. "Woah. Let me guess—she likes *Twilight*.

You can tell. Damn. Why do all these vampire lovers have to be so hot?" He threw the laptop back like a hot potato, all jealous and resentful. "She's out of your league as it stands, Caldo. But don't lose hope. She wants a vampire? Then put some sparkles under your clothes. Like everywhere. By everywhere, I mean your dick. Then, whip out your bedazzled shaft and give her the Edward pout look and say you're an ancient creature. With that, you two are kismet. Don't let her see you walk out into the sun, though. That'll ruin it. At least it did for me."

Fane checked to see if Charles was serious—of course he was. Even Shakespeare's ghost, which haunted these mayonnaise-colored halls, would not be able to tell me whether my life was a tragedy or a comedy.

Act 1: Scene 7

Mine Elder's Most Treasured Shiksa

Finally, it was Bingo night. Er, date night—but it's Friday, so we have to get through Bingo first. The geriatrics don't fuck around about Bingo.

I pulled up to her dorm building and saw a dark angel. The sun shone right on her, a cloud of smoke from her cigarette hovering over her head like a halo. She saw me driving toward her and waved at me with her non-smoking hand. She exhaled and flicked me off playfully. She seemed pretty damn excited to see me. Maybe this really was mutual?

She took one more drag and hopped in the car, her curls going haywire in the best way. Her blush matched her pink shirt. She always looked good, but she looked extra-extra good that day. Mr. Shapiro, an old perv at the retirement home, said she should model if she weren't so short and curvy. He had the right idea, but was misguided.

"Ready for Bingo?" she asked.

"And what comes after."

"Ooo," she cooed. "You're all dressed up."

My cheeks flushed.

"You look good," she added.

"Let's have some fun."

She buckled her seatbelt and I pulled out faster than usual. I wanted to look like a bad boy, but the Honda couldn't keep up and stalled for a second. "Sorry," I said. I flipped off the ignition and turned it on again, moving at a safe speed. "And we're off."

Days of Our Lives reruns rang through the halls like Christmas carols. The place got vacuumed on Fridays, so it smelled extra fresh, and lines moved down the hallway toward the elevator.

We rode our way up to Grandma's and didn't have to knock. She always left it open when she knew I was coming, and that made me feel at home. We peeked inside and found her watching a kitchen show with a man talking to a glazed chicken like a baby while patting breadcrumbs on its legs.

"Hey, Grandma." I walked right in, Alexia following behind me.

Grandma looked away from the TV and held her hands up to welcome us. "My grandson and his beautiful girlfriend."

I rolled my eyes at Alexia like it was no big deal and responded, "Hey, Grandma, it's good to see you. For the first time, you might be right. I am taking Alexia on a date."

Alexia gave me a playful slap on the shoulder. "Stop it. How are you doing, Grandma Goldstein?"

"Alexia, why the secrets about the date? This is wonderful news."

Alexia gave her a side hug. "I haven't seen you since he asked me."

"What does that matter? You should have called me. I thought we were friends."

"You have to go through my publicist," Alexia played like a famous movie star. "But I'll call you next time I have news."

"I like this girl! She's fun. Very sharp. That's a good thing." Grandma had modernized her worldview after my grandpa died. Ever since banana pudding night, she believed us to be the perfect couple who would marry and give her beautiful mixed grandchildren. She wasn't shy to share this and called me like ten times about it.

Alexia winked at me. "Caldo's a real mensch, Grandma Goldstein."

Grandma approved. "I always said Joseph looks like that nice stud actor, Tom Hanks."

"I love Tom Hanks," Alexia agreed.

"I loved him as the handicapped chocolate connoisseur. We watched a film recently called *Castaway*. It was a good film, but oy vey, someone raised the temperature; it was so hot in that rec room—I think the orderlies wanted us to feel like we were on the island with Mr. Hanks and that volleyball."

The loudspeaker that was connected to all the rooms crackled. *Bingo will begin in five minutes in the rec room.*

"That's my cue. I'll see you two inside."

As she walked out, Grandma grabbed my hand. "Are you nervous?"

"What if she doesn't feel like I feel?"

Grandma shooed away my fears with a wave. "You're you, Joseph. That should be enough."

She was the only person in my life who amped me up consistently.

We made our way to the event and found the room

in a ruckus of excitement. Seeing Alexia help set up the tables, I tried to make time go faster. I sped-walked past the rows with all the old people's eyes on me. Getting to the shag carpet by the ball machine, I wiped my brow with the back of my hand.

"No time to dally!" I shouted. "Let's go ahead and start." I smacked the Bingo button so hard the mic shrieked.

"Settle down, kid! I don't even have my card yet!" someone shouted.

Alexia's shoulders shook with laughter. She got all the cards on the table, dodging between a million questions and complaints. "If you have a comment, put it in the suggestion box after the event."

"We got a suggestion box?" a woman with thin magenta hair cried. "Praise God! Finally!"

"She's joking, you dimwit," a man I presumed to be her ex said.

I adjusted the mic again. "Shall we get started?"

"You're still always snarking," the woman shot back. "Never serious. Disgraceful."

"You have a comment?" the ex said. "When don't you have a comment? A comment on this, a comment on that. A Yelp review about it all! Can't you contain yourself?"

"Be respectful!" Grandma Goldstein said. "My Joseph has a date with this young lady, Alexia, and we are holding them up."

"You with him? Are you nuts?" someone shouted at Alexia.

"You have a concussion or something?" that guy's friend added.

I tapped the mic. "Okay. Here we go, now." This was not how I wanted the first date to go, but I tried to make a joke out of it. I picked up the first Bingo ball. I-17, and said, "I-17, as in I'm 17 years old and am going out with a girl who's out of my league."

Chuckles moved in a wave across the room. One lady slapped her knee. "Now, that is funny."

"Don't laugh, Beatrix! He's going to get his heart broke."

"I know," Beatrix hooted, wiping tears. "I can't wait to see it."

Another guy ripped out his dentures and threw them on the table. "Get hurt, Joseph. That's what life is all about."

The room went into a tailspin. One half went bloodthirsty, chanting "Hurt him! Hurt him! Nothing is fair in love and war!" while the other prayed to protect me as if I was in immediate danger.

Someone named Tammy, who had afternoon tea with Grandma, stood and raised her hand. "This isn't all fun and games, Goldstein. I recall you saying Joseph has never had a job. Back in my day, if a man didn't have a job he wasn't dateable. Alexia, I can't blame you if you cancel. You need a provider. You are very attractive and deserve a hard-working man. Joseph, if you want to go on a date, at least get a job at the K-Mart or something."

People nodded their heads in approval and one woman said, "They have very nice bedding and good deals on soap."

Alexia raised her palm. "Excuse me, everyone. Don't I get a say if I go on a date or not?"

Another lady chimed in. "In our heyday, we didn't complain or get divorces, and we had good lives. Young people don't know what is good for them, and I think we can all agree that Joseph would be a good fit for

Alexia. He would cherish her and make sure she stays on the straight and narrow. I am suggesting Alexia goes on a date with him and then they can discuss a job once they settle down."

"With all due respect, that is sort of crazy and very anti-women's. . . everything." Alexia bit her lip. I couldn't help but laugh.

I didn't know what the hell was happening so I smacked the button for another ball. I-4. "Another I. I-4, I-4, as in I-four. . . I. . . for. . .see. . . Grandma, can you do the calls tonight? This is horrible."

Grandma marched to the front like I'd asked her to headline in Vegas. "I sure can. Buckle up, people! You're in for a show!"

Act 1: Scene 8

To Love is to Throw a Pancake at a TERF

We got in my car and I told her while backing out, "I have a place. It's not fancy like the Cheesecake Factory. It's the place of the people."

"Caldo, no McDonald's dates, come on."

"Why are you hating? But it's not McDonald's. It's IHOP."

"IHOP?"

"Yeah, the one in Delray."

"That one's kind of ghetto. Isn't that where prostitutes hang out?"

"Yeah, so what? I'm friends with a few of them."

"IHOP and Denny's are where old AA guys ask me on dates after meetings. But wait. . . how did you become cool with prostitutes at IHOP? You didn't. . ."

"No, I'm not a client. I'm friends with a group of transwomen sex workers—which is the correct way to refer to them."

"You're really weird, Caldo. How did you randomly befriend them at IHOP?" She started laughing while taking another drag. The smoke caught in the evening breeze, hints of menthol and cherry—Alexia's signature blend.

"Mom was driving me nuts before dinner, even though I was doing homework—my English assignment. I said screw this, I'll go to IHOP and do my homework there. When I got there, it was me and a group of women with some killer wigs working the night."

"Did they approach you for a date?"

"Nah. I was trying to finish my paper on *Madame Bovary* while eating pancakes. One of the women came up and said it was her favorite book. I told her I didn't get it and found it boring. She sat me down and schooled me herself."

"What did you learn?"

"Rivera—that's her name—explained that Madame Bovary liked to shop and was lonely for attention, and we're all Madame Bovary. Wanting someone or something to take us away from our shitty situation. She explained it better than my teacher."

"What did you get on the paper?"

"B-plus, and I made friends with some badass bitches. . . their words, not mine. They say hi and ask about school when I'm at IHOP."

"The sad thing about you, Caldo, is you have no friends except sex workers. Which is also the best thing about you. Alright, fine. Take me to IHOP."

I turned right into the Delray Beach IHOP parking lot, feeling nerves vibrate throughout my body. I got out and opened Alexia's door, then mittened my hand around hers.

She gripped tighter. "This is kind of adorable, Caldo."

Not what I wanted to hear, but she didn't let go either.

We walked to the entrance, hands swinging slightly. It felt good—almost too good to be true, but real. Her fingers were cool against mine, her nails occasionally scratching my palm in a way that sent tiny jolts up my arm.

The forty-something hostess recognized me and gave a thumbs-up. "I see you got a new friend. Your other friends are in the back. Sit wherever you'd like, darling."

"Thanks."

The familiar IHOP smell hit me—butter melting into hot griddles, artificial maple syrup, and the slightly burnt edge of overcooked bacon. The place hummed with the clinking of silverware against ceramic plates and the squeak of vinyl booths as people shifted in their seats.

I spotted Rivera and her crew in the back. I waved to the girls drinking coffee and eating eggs. They noticed Alexia, mouths dropping open in awe. Rivera stood up and cranked that Soulja Boy, which I took as approval.

No one else was eating except some older white women with creepy haircuts who were giving Rivera and her friends dirty looks. Very South Florida—people who can't stand each other always end up eating at the same place.

Rivera stopped dancing and signaled me over. "Let's go say hi."

She followed me to Rivera's table, where she sat with Tammy and Delores, returning standoffish glares from a group that may have been TERFs—women who don't like transwomen. South Florida was diverse, which included people who didn't like that it was diverse.

Rivera turned back. The scent of her perfume—something seemingly floral and expensive—wafted toward us. "Look at you, Caldo, on a date, not looking like a serial killer. I like it. Who's this beautiful girl?"

Alexia blushed, pink brightening under the fluorescent lights. She always struggled with compliments—told me she thought everyone was lying. "Thanks. . . I'm Alexia."

"Caldo, you did good. She's fine, and girl, your makeup is done right."

"Thank you, I always try to find that right fit."

"You're not trying. You're doing. You got a good one here too—smart and cute."

I blushed as Alexia grabbed my hand playfully. "He's growing on me."

"Girl, let me do your nails sometime. You're a manicure away from perfection."

"I might take you up on that."

Rivera stood up. "I gotta give you both hugs. You're adorable. Like a WB show walked into IHOP. How long have you known each other?"

Alexia held my hand tighter. "Three months. We became really good friends and Caldo finally asked me out."

"Aw, and he took you to his favorite place," Rivera said. "This is his spot, so you must be special."

"Eh, he's alright. We're going to eat then watch *Gilmore Girls*."

"Oh shit, I love them!" They all started singing the theme song.

After a few lines, a woman at another table screamed, "Excuse me, gentlemen, can you shut the fuck up!" The words hung in the air like a slap.

Shock and hurt hit me. Before I could think of what

to say, Rivera grabbed a pancake plate and screamed, "You did not just gentleman my ass, you snaggletooth TERF!" She threw a pancake that landed smack onto the woman's glasses and bad chunky highlights. It made a wet thwack on impact like a full on Nickelodeon slime blast.

One of Rivera's friends shot syrup that hit another harasser on the chin, sticking like a cheap costume beard. Golden syrup dripped down the woman's neck, disappearing into her collar as she shrieked. The pancake-free bigot-biyotch with a gray mullet grabbed a saltshaker and threw it at our table. It hit the water glass near Alexia, who huddled under the table for cover. The crash of shattering glass joined the symphony of chaos as tiny shards skittered across the tabletop.

Eggs and hash browns flew from both sides. The air became thick with the smell of breakfast foods turned ammunition—yolky, potatoey missiles sailing overhead.

Eggs and hash browns flew from both sides. I ducked to check on Alexia. "Are you okay?"

She covered her head with her arm. "No glass got on me. Is this really happening?"

"Food fight!" a manager screamed.

I grabbed Alexia's hand. "Duck and run! Let's get out of here!"

We kept our heads down and ran toward the exit holding hands. A hash brown grazed my ear, still hot enough to sting as grease smeared across my temple, but we made it to the door while food kept flying. It felt surreal yet romantic as we ran out and got back into my car. We slammed the doors shut, panting, the smell of breakfast battle clinging to our clothes. All I could think was: I didn't know if this was the worst or best date ever.

Act 1: Scene 9

Ye Chariot Doth Speedeth (Riding Dirty on I-95)

I drove out of the parking lot while Alexia was cracking up in the passenger seat. The adrenaline pumping through me leveled out, and I started laughing with her when we hit a red light. Only in South Florida would something like this happen before seven.

Alexia was cracking up. "That was fucking nuts, Caldo!"

"Totally surreal," I said. "I don't think I've ever been in a food fight."

"Me either, but those assholes deserved to be hit with pancakes. People are awful and rude. I can't believe they threw a saltshaker!"

The light turned green, and I responded, "Yeah, fuck 'em. That said, I was hoping for something a little more romantic. Sorry you almost got hit by a saltshaker."

"That's what you get for taking a girl to IHOP instead of The Cheesecake Factory." She gave my arm a playful squeeze. "I'm playing, Caldo. That was kind of awesome. Definitely the most interesting thing that's happened to me since I've been sober."

I wasn't sure about what to do for dinner, maybe going to The Cheesecake Factory, but Alexia said, "Why don't we go back to my place where it's safe and boring? I can make some mac and cheese and then put on some *Gilmore Girls*."

"That sounds pretty great."

"Cool," she said as I drove to Boca Raton. It felt so good that she wanted to hold my hand. The Beatles might be the most Boomer band ever, but they understood how special hand-holding could be.

This felt like a moment I'd only seen in movies. Where the person you always wanted maybe might want you back. She put her fingers on top of mine and told me, "I'm actually having a really good time, Caldo."

"Me too."

"Good. I feel like I know you pretty well, but there's stuff I don't know."

Feigning calmness, I replied, "What do you want to know? I'm an open book."

"So like, you never tell me what you want to do, or study when you get to college, or if you even want to go to college. What's Joseph Caldo's secret dream that no one knows about?"

In a weird way, being intimate felt as scary as sex. Maybe they really were connected. I took a deep breath and told her something I hadn't even told Heller. "I want to do something with film. Not be a critic or argue on Reddit or YouTube comments like I do now, but do something behind a camera. But it's complicated. It's hard to explain."

"Why don't you make a film for fun? I'd act for you if you wrote and directed something."

The prospect of filming Alexia inspired a surge of possibilities. But right on cue, the whim got squashed by memories of my mother's damnation—I couldn't do anything right. "I can't. It's a long story. Mom wants me to learn to code. I guess I'll do that."

"You can be a filmmaker, Caldo. You can be whatever you want. If you want to code then do your thing. But it sounds to me like what you really need is some life experience."

As I turned into FAU, she put her hand on my cheek as if she wanted to soothe me. It worked. Maybe she was right. Feeling her touch, all things felt possible. But it felt scary, too. Friendship was drifting away and something much bigger was growing between us.

Act 1: Scene 10

In Favor of the Noble Jess

We got out of the car, and my nerves were going haywire. She walked toward me, and our hands felt like magnets drawn to each other as they wrapped around each other again. Fit like mittens. There had always been this nice comfort between us that made all of this easier. I'd felt at home with her ever since the fart attack at the retirement home. Damn, that fart might have been the best wingman ever. Amore Fate, as Miss Connie liked to say—or more like Amore Farte: to love the fates and farts.

The ocean wind blew toward us as we reached her apartment door. My nerves only got heavier and harder, and it hit me that I'd never been inside a girl's room before. Alexia was also not a girl—she was like a legal woman.

She took out her keys and opened the door. It smelled like candles from Bed Bath & Beyond. It was a two-bedroom apartment, more than a dorm, with a little kitchen and a bathroom. One of the doors was open.

Alexia inspected the room. "Good. My roommate isn't here. She is probably at a sorority meeting or something."

She sounded happy about this, and I was feeling ecstatic, but said with false nonchalance, "That's cool."

"My bedroom is to the right. You can wait there. I'll be in the kitchen."

I did what she said even though I was freaking out. Her room was a contrast to how I assumed it would be —organized and decorated with meaningful relics. Cube shelves were lined with photobooth pictures and letters from family and friends. Clothes were folded and put away in order. A floppy stuffed rabbit sat on a clean, well-made bed. On the nightstand, she had one of those mosaic-looking lamps you can buy in Morocco or, at the very least, from your local incense store. I took off my shoes and placed them by the door to match her unexpected formality. A sticky-noted, dog-eared copy of *Twelve Steps* sat readily on a bookshelf next to a row of sobriety coins.

This was a real woman! Complex and mature. Someone who lived and liked sex. I thanked God my feet didn't reek or anything and waited for her, lounging on her bed. I tried to look carefree with my body language, but I couldn't hide the truth—I was nervous as fuck. I felt like I should have been doing something, so I climbed around for the remote. No luck, so I forced my focus on finding *Gilmore Girls*. I dug through a bin until I found the Season Three Blu-ray case. Empty! Stupid me. I'd overthought it. Of course it was already in the player. This girl was obsessed. I pushed play and waited for the menu music to start.

The song felt really emotional, or maybe it was me who was emotional because I didn't want my life to be over and wanted the opposite of death. I wanted to feel the most alive I could with Alexia, which would mean losing my virginity to Alexia tonight. The college girl, Alexia. The girl, woman, whatever she was, who I'd had a crush on since the fart attack, Alexia. The person who was basically my best friend, Alexia. Alexia. Damn.

The theme music ended, and I started to smell cheese. Never had the smell of heated cheese been so intermingled with my thoughts of sex. The mac and cheese smell got stronger, and Alexia arrived with two bowls.

She handed me a bowl and sat by me on the bed. "Yes, I love this episode." She moved back to the headboard. "It's cool—eat here. I basically eat almost every meal in bed."

I followed her lead and got comfortable sitting close to her. I blew on the mac and cheese and took the first bite.

"Damn, that's really good."

"I know, right. I make some dope mac and cheese," she said proudly and slid a little closer to me. If heaven existed, it would be eating mac and cheese while you were lying next to your crush.

The bowls cooled down, and we ate pretty fast. It was like the food was getting in the way of our arms being wrapped around each other. We finished the last of it and placed the empty bowls on her nightstand.

I lay back down, and she lay in the crook of my arm. We snuggled closer, letting our bodies drift into one another. The episode played while I began to lightly rub her shoulders and arms. It was intense to touch her so softly, and so was this episode. This girl, Rory, was deciding if she should be with Dean, the Blockbuster guy, or this guy, Jess, who was an art film nerd like me.

Wow, I was giving a shit about the goddamn *Gilmore Girls*.

Alexia was engrossed as we watched Rory finally pick Jess. I wanted to scream 'yes!' but instead looked at her and asked, "Why do you think she picks him over that Dean dude? He is taller and way better looking and all that stuff. Like, why pick Jess—he's kind of weird, annoying, and a pain in the ass."

"Dean is definitely hot—hotter than Jess, but here is the thing: Rory and Jess, they have a connection. They have something special." She scooted even closer. "Sometimes, the connection matters way more."

Act 1: Scene 11

Of Dubstep Most Wicked

The credits rolled and we sat there like idiots. The TV screen was still glowing blue, and our breathing had gotten all quiet and deliberate. Deliberate for me, at least. I don't know what she was thinking. I synced my exhales with the whir of the disc player. We sat there for so long that the whirring eventually stopped. The TV made the usual beep-boop sound before falling into sleep mode.

"It's so dark," I said in the most attractive voice I could muster.

The bass bumped from another dorm room down the hall. Ping pong balls ricocheted off rackets to the beat. "You know I love me some dubstep, but I've been staying away from partying in any form."

She looked so sad. She deserved to party, and all I wanted was to make her laugh. "Dubstep sounds like robot farts."

It worked. Then she leaned her body closer to mine and collapsed in my arms. "Beep boop," she said. "Just like the TV."

"Beep boop," I said back. I looked into her big, dark eyes. All this time, I'd wanted the kiss to be perfect. I'd envisioned myself at golden hour—wearing a collared white shirt with the spice of an Altoid on my breath. But lying there in the dens of ramen packets, instant coffees, and community showers was even better. My head moved forward, and our lips finally met.

Woah. It was even better than the movies made it out to be.

We kept kissing, finding a rhythm as I followed her tongue. Then, she followed my tongue. Were we playing tag? Cat and mouse? Duck, Duck, Goose? Who cares—it was badass.

Then I went for Hide and Seek, reaching in the dark for her every part. Instincts I didn't even know I had kicked in, touching her in ways I didn't even know I could touch someone. Our clothes were coming off, and we were kissing each other's necks, shoulders, and chests. Alexia's bra came off, and my God.

I didn't know whether to touch or kiss them, so I did both. My body moved ahead of my mind like I was a sensual superhero. I drove the motorboat straight into the fold and didn't even blow a raspberry. She started kissing my chest back, then inched her hand lower, slower. The suspense.

I was harder than a stale baguette, praying the thing wouldn't shatter into crumbs. Before a boy becomes a man, he worries women will think his dick is pathetic. She didn't say anything of the sort and ran her hand all along it.

She paused. It was happening. I'd traveled to the Netherlands.

I remembered I was supposed to rub around the clit area. Clockwise. Right? It was clockwise? I couldn't see anything. Her hair moved across my eyes like windshield wipers, our breath humidifying. Finally, I felt an opening and put a finger inside. She giggled, and not in a mean way. She pulled back to look at me, then kissed the tip of my nose. I think she really liked me.

We continued to kiss, everything faster this time. I practically launched my mouth between her thighs and almost wished she'd use them to squeeze my brains out. Forget all the advice I'd annotated on those websites. Never mind all that choreography I'd memorized on porn. I had the real thing right there and let me tell you —it was unsanctimonious.

I started licking like a Neanderthal—no ideas, only instinct. This was the right choice. She literally moaned, which I understood was a coveted utterance. Then, she became a conductor. "A little faster. Higher. More rhythm. Steady. Like that."

My jaw went stiff then numb. I needed anesthesia! I laid my cheek on her inner thigh like a pillow and closed my eyes for a moment, breathless.

But she grabbed me by the hair and pulled me back up. I felt endeared by her messiness, cracking up as I pulled a strand of hair that was stuck to her lip gloss. We caught air for a second, then she whispered quietly, as if anyone could hear us or cared, "I'll get us a condom."

Consider me heartwarmed. Cupid wielded no arrows but gave pats on the head.

When she stood up, I noticed my eyes had finally adjusted and, cowabunga, it hit me how naked she was. No clothes, not even a sock. When she bent over to pull a condom from the drawer, my penis went teleseismic. If I couldn't last more than twenty seconds, I was going to kill myself. It was settled. But wait—hallelujah—I remembered my depression meds made it hard to come. That side effect in conjunction with being depressed in the first place made my outlook good.

"A blue Trojan," I said. "Ribbed for your pleasure."

She rolled her eyes playfully. "Can I try something?" But before I could answer, she unwrapped it and put it on me with her mouth. What the fuck was happening? People actually did that? Real people?

I crawled on top of her and kissed the tip of her nose like she'd done to mine. Then, I became certain I was totally in love and knew without a doubt I would be with her forever. I was one of those guys who would only have one woman for their whole entire life and be thrilled about it.

She put me inside of her, and for the first time I truly understood why every bard from Shakespeare to Flo Rida was obsessed with getting it on.

Act 1: Scene 12

What Follows Passion's End

My chemical sadness and the pills for which to treat said chemical sadness did their duties, and the act lasted a good, long while. It was the best virginity loss story I'd ever heard of, and it was mine.

Then came the best part—spooning a girl. I'd never admit it to my imaginary bro friends, but come on. Sex isn't about sex—it's about what comes after. A naked little spoon whose scent is everywhere around you and you never want to shower again because of it.

This should have been the most perfect moment of my life, but as I held her close, I got that swallowed-a-cherry-pit feeling like I was about to cry. Why was I like this, sentimentalizing every instance before it was even a memory? I got too vulnerable and my heart—my damn stupid heart—felt like an open wound against her back.

What the hell was happening? I was a straight-as-fuck high school dude who just lost his virginity to a super hot college girl. I should've felt euphoric—a

Buddhist achieving nirvana—but she wasn't some girl. I'd been afflicted by affection.

I missed the moment before it ever passed, mourning it like a forgotten detail in the mind of some demented elderly man playing Bingo at the retirement home. I didn't want my joy to spoil, but it curdled and soured in the heat of the truth that I wanted so much more than sex.

I wanted a girlfriend. I wanted a relationship. I wanted her to feel it, too.

The question made me sick—what if she didn't feel the same?

She saw it in my expression. "Hey, what is it? What's going on?"

"I don't know."

She pulled a pillow over her eyes then peeked out. "What do you mean? That was nice."

Then, my throat caught on fire and I totally exploded. "That was more than nice. That was—that was perfect." My tone sounded angry, or maybe like a plea. A child begging to be taken to the zoo. I became crazy. "Alexia, I love you. I'm so in love with you."

She squinted her green eyes, getting serious fast. I waited for a smile to return, dying for any indication she understood what I said and felt it too. But there was nothing. If anything, she looked worried.

"Oh, Caldo. Shit. This wasn't—this wasn't supposed to be that."

"Supposed to be what?"

"You think this is love?" she asked. There wasn't any mockery in her voice. Her eyes started to water. She covered them with her hands.

"You have feelings for me, right? Love is a scary word. But something?" She stayed quiet for so long it felt like the line went dead. There was my answer. My eyes stung, too. "I'm an idiot. Nevermind me." I shrugged and forced a self-deprecating half-smile.

"I'm so sorry. Did I fuck up? I mean, I want to date right now, I'm not looking for a relationship."

"No, I don't regret this." But wait. What? "Are you dating other people?"

"Well yeah, just some guy from AA. It's what adults do. Ah man, I fucked up."

"I fucked up, I should've said I was a virgin and asked if you were dating anyone."

"Oh fuck, Caldo. Why didn't you tell me you were a virgin?"

My brain finally caught up and translated what this meant—*I don't feel the same as you. This isn't special to me in the way it is for you. This was a hookup with a friend, nothing more, nothing less.* My heart broke. Tears came, for real, and I hated myself for letting them flow. "But you feel something too, right? Anything? Can I get any confirmation that you care about me? Maybe even love me."

"I do love you. You're sweet and funny. You're a great friend. I wanted to see what was here, but I didn't know how you felt. I thought this was fun. I hope you did, too? But now I see you're feeling more than that. Damn. I don't know what to say."

It was clear my stupid movie analogy was some immature romanticization that had no bearing on reality. I wasn't her indie heartthrob—a friend with benefits for a bored college freshman who couldn't drink.

"I gotta stop doing shit like this. I screw up every good friendship that is worth anything. I really screw up anything that is good." She seemed to be saying this to herself as much as to me. She was being too hard on herself and the really crappy thing was she meant it.

I wanted to offer her anything but felt stuck in my own hurt and disappointment. She was a good friend, but it wasn't the time to say that. At least not for me.

"I'm sorry, Caldo, but we gotta not see each other for a while. This was a bad idea."

"Come on. Please," I begged, feeling pathetic.

"No—this is what I do. It's all over my Fourth Step. We need to take a break."

"Wait, wait. . ." I said, trying one last time to change her mind or at least make her understand. "Why not me, Alexia? Why don't you see me as a boyfriend who could really love you and treat you right?"

"Ah Caldo, don't do this. Come on. . ."

"Why Alexia, why don't you feel this too?"

"Because I want someone who is confident and knows themselves and isn't going to fall in love the first time they are intimate with someone. We are not meant to be this and I'm stopping it so we can maybe one day be friends again."

Ouch. The pain entered my bloodstream and flowed through my whole body.

We went to opposite sides of the room and put our clothes back on, still in the dark. I imagined a garish lamp turning on, shifting the scene into a nightmare. But we stayed in the melancholy—cloudy and surreal. Even the beer pong party down the hall had seized. The worst feeling was knowing this would never happen again. Not just the sex, but the kissing and cuddling and being able to talk. Spooning. I wish being clothed had made me feel better, but it didn't. Her back was to me, and it hurt. It really hurt. I was only a dumb boy. I couldn't even say goodbye.

I pushed out of the dorm and cry-walked to my car. The ocean breeze chilled my tears as dubstep choruses circulated like chasms in the university pocket. I couldn't start the ignition. I just sat there and wished I had someone to talk to about this. I felt like I didn't have anyone.

Act 1: Scene 13

In The Dawn Most Sorrowful, A Father's Rib

I woke up in my car, startled by loud-as-hell honking. Through the blur and crust of tears, I saw the sunrise breaking through—a pink grapefruit in the deep blue-black of dawn. I looked behind me, and there was a group of frat boys in a Jeep honking their horn and cursing at me.

I rubbed my eyes and cranked the window down and screamed at the frat boys, "My crush just took a hammer to my fucking heart. I'm going—just wait a minute!"

These dudes could beat the shit out of me, but I probably sounded and looked nuts, so they backed off, waiting for me to drive away. I was pissed off to be back in reality, where the sadness was mixing with anger.

I started the car, and the radio was still on the 80s soul jams station. I liked how that one never had commercial breaks. They were only playing for themselves.

The anger morphed back into sadness, and I started

crying again. I backed out as frat boys flipped me off and called me a crazy-ass pussy.

I drove out of the FAU parking lot, back onto Glades Road. My thoughts went from the pain of remembering what Alexia said to my pain-in-the-ass mother, who I knew was freaking out in my absence. Shit, I hoped she didn't call the police, but she did know about the date with Alexia.

The cars slowed to a stop, and I saw an accident ahead. To my right was an old couple who also had their windows down, with an old lady in the passenger seat telling her husband, "Watch out for the boy next to us—his eyes are very red! He is on the drugs!" She was terrified.

"No, I'm not on drugs. I'm cut up by a girl."

"Murray, he said he isn't on drugs, but freshly rejected!"

"I heard him, Martha," the man said, concentrating on the road. "You'll live, kid."

I started to tear up again. "It doesn't feel like I will!"

"This is dangerous. Oy, pay attention," the wife said. "You're driving, not a dating counselor. Oh look, there is the accident."

"Love is dangerous, kid, but everything worthwhile is," he said as we all inched slowly toward the accident.

They passed me, and I checked my phone to see if Alexia had texted or called, but there were only twenty calls from Mom. Not an exaggeration—actually, maybe twenty-two—and about the same amount of texts.

I drove and drove, thinking about last night and what I was going to tell Mom, until I pulled into my driveway and parked next to Mom's blue Jeep.

I stumbled out of the car and clenched my keys. I reached the door and unlocked it as quietly as humanly possible, hoping she wouldn't hear, but right after the click I heard Mom scream, "Joseph! Joseph! Joseph, is that you?"

"Yeah, Mom. It's me," I said, taking a deep breath to prepare for the hurricane of neuroticism.

She was sitting there in the living room like a prison guard. She stood up from the couch with worry, anger, and relief battling in her eyes. "Why didn't you call? I was getting ready to call the police!"

"I should have called. I'm sorry. It—"

She cut me off and continued, "There are gangs in Palm Beach County! Did you know that? The Ten O'Clock News says the Diamond Folk Nation is on the rise! And your eyes are so red—do you have angel dust eyes?"

"Angel, what?"

"Drugs!"

"No, I don't do drugs. You know that. Dr. Heller said they'd mess up the meds."

"Well then what the hell happened?"

Enter: Dad. Much calmer, but I could tell he was concerned. He yawned. "Joseph, why didn't you call? You're supposed to call, son. You know that. Your mother even called your grandma, and she said you were with Alexia." He paused and asked, "Oh—did you spend the night with her?" He looked like he needed to toot due to nerves as he approached Mom on the couch.

"Really, you and Alexia? You both—"

Dad laid his hand on her shoulder. She squeezed it, a break for some love, before they returned to me with their secondhand rue.

Her disbelief was a reminder of the harsh truth of my parents thinking I wasn't good enough for Alexia, and I began to cry again.

"What? What did I say, Joseph? He needs new medication, Robert. Look at him. You need to talk to Dr. Hell—and it's time you get a job, or I'm taking the car away, enough is enough—"

My father cut her off calmly. "Honey, why don't you go make some breakfast. Joseph and I can talk while the ESPN pregame gets started."

"Oy, I'm going to go get some sleep. You two can make your own breakfast—I'm too tired and full of nerves," she said, getting up. "Later I'm setting up an interview for you, Joseph. You need a job to learn to be a man of responsibility. No more free rides to see your shiksa slut!"

"Come on, Joey, let's go to the living room and put on the pregame," Dad said, putting his hand on my shoulder. I felt the weight of his wide palm and fingers sinking into my shoulder, and even though this blatant patronizing should annoy me, I found it weirdly soothing.

I followed him to the living room. He sat on the couch and turned on the TV. The same group of guys that traveled around to different colleges with people yelling and putting up weird signs were raising hell in the background. This already felt super awkward. With football stuff being on, it made it easier or more masculine? I didn't know.

"Joseph, you really should have called. You know how your mother gets."

"I know, I know."

"She loves you. She just worries."

"I know."

"What happened with Alexia?"

I got teary-eyed again. "I don't really want to talk about it."

"Look, if it's sex stuff, we are both going to hate talking about it, but you look really upset."

I wiped my eyes. "We had sex. Okay, we did. And I lost my virginity."

"Um, wait. You're upset about that?" Dad asked. I've seen pictures. She is quite the—"

"And then I told her I loved her. Okay. I told her how I felt, and she doesn't feel the same, and she freaked out. And now she doesn't even want to be friends. She wants a total break."

Dad was dumbfounded. "Darn. That's—that's pretty rough."

"I thought she might feel the same, but—" I started crying again. This was almost more mortifying than last night, but I was too tired to hide it.

Dad wasn't a hugger, but he put his hand on my shoulder again. "Yeah, that would hurt, but I'm sure it hurts for her too."

"I doubt it. She has like a million guys who want to date her. She'll probably be dubstepping with some douchebag in a week."

"Your generation calls sex dubstepping?"

"No, it's crappy music Alexia likes. Ugh, why does this hurt so much?"

"It just does, Joey. It just does."

"Do you think it hurts for her too?"

"Yes. I had to stop working and being friends with someone who had feelings for me, and it was hard. It hurt."

I sat back, feeling a little shocked. "Really, Dad? Who?"

"Do you remember my assistant Alison?"

"Yeah, she was nice. She cleaned my teeth once. What happened to her?"

"Well, there was a reason why she left. She liked me."

The shock that someone else could like my dad made my tears stop. "Uh. What?"

"It's true. She did. She confessed she was in love with me."

"Woah."

"Woah is right, son. She was beautiful, intelligent, and funny. But she didn't have my rib, so to speak."

"Not having your rib? What?"

"It's something your grandpa Goldstein told me before your mother and I were going to get married. It was a parable related to the story of Adam and Eve. Your grandfather said that God took one of Adam's ribs to create Eve. I had already heard this at Sunday School, but he explained that according to science, men have one less rib than women."

"That doesn't sound true, Dad. That sounds totally inaccurate, like scientifically."

"That's not the point."

"What's the point?"

"The point is, he told me that for every man, there is some woman who has his rib, and he has to find that woman. I smiled at your grandfather and told him that I knew without a doubt that your mother had my rib."

We both paused. "This really is sexist and heteronormative, but also kind of nice. I wish I knew Grandpa Goldstein more. Still can't believe he was a rabbi."

Dad teared up, staring at the screen. "He was a good rabbi, even if he didn't move with the times. Look, take your grandfather's little parable to heart. Know that there is someone out there for you, and I know it hurts. It sounds like Alexia doesn't have your rib, but have faith you'll find someone who does."

ACT 2

Act 2: Scene 1

Marquis de Sade's School of Hard Knocks

Monday morning. Monday effing morning. Driving my stupid car to my stupid school. Two days after THE DAY. The day I kept reliving over and over again. And the days after THE DAY, checking for any texts and Facebook messages from Alexia. Nothing.

I felt super unsexy and uncool that day, not because of Alexia's rejection but because I was wearing those lame JC Penney interview clothes. There were some guys that could pull off the dress shirt and khakis thing, and I wasn't one of them. I looked like if LinkedIn was a person. Mom had said a million times that she'd take the car away if I didn't go to the job interview and visit Grandma after school, so I was going to do both. I needed my damn car. It was the last remaining shred of autonomy, masculinity, and self-respect I had.

I kept wondering—ok, maybe obsessing—about the possibility of seeing Alexia again at the retirement home. What was that even going to feel like? I fantasized about her seeing me eating my pudding next to my grandma and realizing she felt the same as me. That she was scared of love, but like the banana pudding they served at 4:30 dinner—it was fake, packed with sugar that led to a crash and a stomachache. I'd never share that feeling with her again therefore I was broken.

Dread washed over me while pulling into the school parking lot. I really didn't want to deal with Fane or Charles or any of my school's bullshit that day. I didn't want to deal with anything that day. I should have stayed home or pretended to be sick. I felt sick. I didn't feel right. I had struggled to sleep. It hurt, and it took all my strength not to text or call Alexia. The worst part was there was still a part of me that thought she'd give me another chance, while another voice kept telling me I was never good enough for her to begin with.

I parked my car in front of the playground area. My legs felt stiff. I'd never gotten drunk, but I assumed this was what a hangover felt like. I opened the gate to the kids screaming and yelling on the playground. I stumbled toward the school's back door, not wanting to get teased by them like they usually did.

I tried to sneak past the playground but I heard a little boy say, "Ha, look at the older boy, he's walking like he pooped his pants."

"Ha! He's a poop butt!" some kid said.

The girls and boys chanted, "Poop pants! Poop pants! Eating poop in Paris, France!"

I stopped and looked at the little bastards. I gave them a stare of death. "Shut your goddamn mouths! I didn't poop my pants. The truth is a girl that I loved, yes loved. LOVED. SHE! Pooped! On my fucking heart! And one day it will happen to you. It will happen to all of you! You'll all get your hearts pooped on!"

"Joseph Caldo!" I heard from the open back door

entrance and saw it was Miss Connie. "Unless you are discussing Marquis de Sade, there will be no mention of horrid acts of defecation to children. Get inside, you are late and acting like a deviant philistine!"

"They started it!" I said making a gangsta 'what's up' sign to the boys.

Miss Connie led me in through the school's back door. I followed her into my room feeling frustrated, emo, and angry.

Those stupid kids making fun of me stung, because they thought I was a loser, and it sucked because little kids could spot that stuff. I never had a shot with Alexia. Our hookup was that SAT word, an anomaly. I bit my lip so I wouldn't cry in front of Miss Connie.

"Mr. Caldo, that wasn't wise. You will be reading to them later this week and I have something special in store for that reading."

"Shit, that's right."

"Language!"

"Sorry."

"Mr. Caldo, you have never berated or even engaged with the children next door. Are things—are you okay?"

"No, it feels like I'm dying."

"Oh, dear. I didn't know you had medical problems."

"Dying, like metaphorically."

"Ah yes, teenage heartache, the poetry genre that never goes away."

"God. Miss Connie. This is serious. This hurts so bad! Ugh, I relate and now get all those emo-poets you keep making me read."

"The Romantics?"

"Yeah, those tools."

"Byron was not a 'tool,' Joseph. And Rilke was a beautiful poetic man; you know him and Nietzsche ended up loving the same girl, Lou Andreas-Salomé. Both were very different men, with different philosophies, but both found love in one woman who didn't love either of them back."

"No wonder Nietzsche thought everything sucked. I had a Lou Salomé too, and her name was Alexia. And she rejected me too, and I don't even have a stupid mustache or lame poems to show for it."

Miss Connie laughed. "Sorry. I have empathy for you, Joseph. It's very hard. Especially the first time."

"The worst thing about it is I can't accept that it's over."

"Well, half of literature focuses on this theme."

"I think biology has got this stuff down more."

"I think Shakespeare would beg to differ!"

"What's his deal, like why is Shakespeare the Lady Gaga of plays?"

"He is something much more than that, Mr. Caldo. He captures what you're feeling. I think your next assignment should be on Shakespeare and the subject of love. I think you're ready to learn something that only Shakespeare can teach."

Act 2: Scene 2

Enter Valentina, Stage Right

It was lunchtime and I wasn't even a little bit hungry. I looked at the gluten-free protein bar Mom had packed for me and dropped it on the table. Time dripped by until there was a knock and Jamie came in, like she did every damn day, "Are you mad at me? Caldo, do you think the world is coming to an end? Are you eating a cheese sandwich today? Do you think Fane is planning on attacking me today? Do you think it's going to rain today?"

"You know what? I don't feel like answering your questions today."

"But how will I know if you are mad at me? Caldo, do you think—"

"No, okay. No to all. No. No. No. No. And no. There Jamie. No. Okay?"

"Ok. Can I eat here? I feel scared about Fane, and I think you are wrong. I think she is going to do something very bad to me today."

"I don't care."

Before she could pipe up again, there was another knock on the door. "What do you want?" I yelled.

Connie and a new girl walked into the room.

"Oof. Sorry, Miss Connie."

Wait. I recognized her. This was the girl Fane had described as looking like Amish J-Lo—the new student she'd mentioned last week. Except now I could see what she'd meant. Behind those oversized glasses and frumpy clothes, there was something there.

The new girl had this I'm-better-than-everyone-at-this-school vibe. Which might have been true, but it made me not like her right off the bat. Normal and well-put-together people didn't belong at this school. She also reminded me of the drug reps that came to Grandma's retirement home; she had the same unshakeable confidence even without the designer outfit.

"Jamie, it's so nice to see you socializing, but Mr. Caldo has to go read right now." Miss. Connie said.

I put my head down. "I'm not up for this. Can't I do this next week?" I went back to staring down into the void that was my white desk.

"Mr. Caldo, please look up. You will not be alone. I have decided to get Miss Diaz involved with you right away and help you out. As part of our new peer mentoring initiative—which is a requirement for Valentina's scholarship—she'll be working with struggling students. Valerie is doing college-level AP English and will also be doing some TAing with me as well."

I looked up at the new chick. "What are you? Some kinda genius?"

The new girl looked embarrassed, her big brown eyes shy behind her glasses.

"Mister Caldo, apologize right now."

"My bad. Whatevs." I really felt the apathy and depression starting to kick in. Maybe I was a Shakespeare play instead of an art film. Just a sad-ass Shakespeare play no one really liked except Boomers, like Miss Connie and lit nerds. I wasn't even good enough to be a shitty art film.

"Miss Diaz, I apologize for Mr. Caldo. He thinks that because he has girl problems he can act like a ruffian."

"A ruffian?" I wasn't even sure what that meant. "Okay. Again. My bad."

"Mr. Caldo, do not ever use the phrase 'my bad' again. Please give her a sincere apology using the formal English language."

"Okay, okay-ay-yay. I apologize, Valentina." I stood up. "Alright, fine, let's get this over with."

"You can call me Valerie." Valerie seemed confused and tried to play it cool. "Anyway, let's go do what Miss Connie wants."

"The mentoring program is quite simple," Miss Connie continued. "Miss Diaz, you will help Mr. Caldo improve his academic performance, starting with a creative performance project on Shakespeare's romantic themes. Think of it as intensive tutoring with accountability on both sides."

"Both sides?" Valerie asked, worried.

"Yes, Miss Diaz. Your scholarship renewal depends on measurable improvement in your assigned student. I always thought it would be Charles or Fane, but I see now, Mr. Caldo, you are the one who needs the most help."

"Him?" Valerie said in shock. "Wait. I thought I'd be tutoring the children. They are so much more motivated and stable. No offense."

"None taken. It's true. Have her help the kids. I'm already a lost cause."

"I see the potential in both of you," Miss Connie said with that scary determination in her eyes. "This will work."

"If you say so," I shrugged.

"Finish your lunch, Mr. Caldo, and Valerie, let me give you a tour, but before the end of the day I want you to have started the mentor program, which can be during and after school."

Act 2: Scene 3

Wherein Our Hero Stalks His Ex Whilst Genius Girl Roasts Him

There was a lot I could do today to try to get back on track. Maybe take the mentor thing seriously, or actually go to Biology class with Mr. Wilkins, but instead I hid out in Michelle's room and stalked Alexia's Facebook.

Her profile picture was still the same—her at some party before she got sober, munching on whipped cream while painted with attractive rave girl stuff. This was less about longing, which would have been less pathetic, but more about trying to figure out who else she was dating. There was a check-in on Saturday at a nice coffee spot in Boca Raton, The Funky Buddha. That was not post-AA stuff, that was a date. Oh my god, she probably saw the other guy to console her the day after!

I kept scrolling through her photos like I was picking at a scab. Pictures of her at AA meetings. Pictures of her looking healthy and glowing. Pictures that didn't include me at all, like our entire relationship had been a brief detour in her real life.

I wanted to comment on something, anything, to remind her I existed. But what would I even say? "Hey, remember when we had sex and I ruined everything?"

Michelle was eating a kosher ham sandwich, looking down at an unfinished puzzle. Her overly-focused eyes while eating a nice kosher sandwich reminded me of the retirement home when they all worked on Sudoku during their extra early dinner.

"Oh man, I'm going to see her today, Michelle. It's going to be mortifying," I told her and dropped my head down on the table.

"What are you doing in here?" a voice of judgment spoke. "Mr. Wilkins is waiting for you and Connie said I needed to find you. Are you napping here. . . oh sorry, I'm Valerie, good to meet you."

I lifted my head up to see Michelle not acknowledging Valerie but staring at her sandwich.

"She's. . ."

"I understand. . ." Valerie responded, still giving a friendly smile toward Michelle. She turned her attention to me and frowned. "I don't know how you play hooky at a one on one tutoring school. It's almost impressive how bad at school you are."

"Thanks?"

She rolled her eyes and said, "Alright, so either go back to class or let's figure out this Shakespeare project. I don't fail at anything, and if a bunch of white boys can get famous whining and quoting lines about their breakups, you can do the same with Shakespeare."

"Why you gotta hate on Fall Out Boy. Those are good songs."

"Yeah, for babies."

"Jesus, you're a ball of sunshine."

"And you're a pain in my ass, so stop whining and

let's make sure you do this project and you act like less of a ruffian, which is a vibe I don't feel from you, but cursing at children is a red flag."

"They started it."

"Oh boy. This is going to be harder than the SAT, but I got a 1500 and you got a participation award."

Valerie was definitely a. . . I don't want to use the b word, but it's the only word that would come to me. I saw why she won debate competitions. But was the goal of a good debate to make the opposition feel bad? Because my mind drifted to the future when I would call Bingo while the old folks said I told you so.

I wanted a protector, okay fine, a bitch. A bitch who was a master debater in my corner who could make anyone of any age be silenced by a sentence. Also, maybe it would miraculously make Alexia jealous to see me with a smart alpha femme nerd. "I'll do this mentor thing if you come with me to volunteer at a nursing home and make sure the old Jews don't make me cry."

"What?"

"I'll explain in the car after school, it's for the Shakespeare project. I can give you a ride."

"Fine, I'll let my mom know I have a ride home."

Act 2: Scene 4

To Rideth I-95 with Valerie

While I drove Valerie down I-95 to the nursing home and explained all that happened it felt like I was talking about somebody else. Sharing my problems with Valerie as we sped down I-95, I felt as if I was detailing my own troubles from the outside. As if my life was a horror film that you know stuck the landing because someone in the theatre uttered an audible WTF when the credits popped up at the end.

I made a right turn and got off the exit with Valerie sitting in the passenger seat uncomfortably silent. It was weird to just drop all this personal stuff: love, sex, and heartbreak on a girl my age who is a total stranger. She shrugged and finally said, "You sound like my debate club friend after she hooked up with a proper Fuck Boy. Maybe feminism is working. . . seeing the role reversal happen. A lot of girls lose their virginity like this, it doesn't make you special."

My "mentor" had acted like I told her the summary of some lame movie. "I kind of shared the most mortifying thing that has happened in my life, which is saying something. You can't even commiserate, or is your love life perfect like your GPA?"

She stared at her phone. "Sorry, but I'm not going to talk about my love life with some weird emo guy I met today, mentor or not. You still haven't explained why going to the retirement home is going to help our Shakespeare project."

"Would you be mad if I admitted I lied and needed someone like you to enter the room with me? As stand-in arm candy? They literally made bets that she'd reject me!"

I expected her to get mad, but she started laughing. Her usual annoyed frown returned. "What do you mean someone like me?"

"Um. You know. Someone who is going to make sure I'm not mocked by three different generations." Yikes. I was so out of sorts that when we passed by my shrink's office, it seemed like a worthy pit stop. "Anyway, stay by my side and make sure the old Jewish men don't make fun of me too much. You look normal. So act normal."

"Wow. Normal looking. Fake arm candy. Thank you for that."

"You know what I mean! Also, can you call Bingo so I don't have to?"

She snorted. "Bingo? Is this your unpaid job or mine?"

"It's so awkward."

"Can't you skip a day? You're in a mental health crisis."

"My mom will have a fit."

"It's too much, Caldo. Don't you have an interview after this, too?"

"Yeah. K-Mart."

"And you'd make actual money there?"

"Define actual. It's minimum wage, okay? I have to fulfill my prophecy of being a spoiled, lazy white guy."

Act 2: Scene 5

To Have Heartache is to Live in the Junkyard

Valerie admired the welcoming hall. "Damn, this is fancy."

It was on the higher end of nursing homes with the entrance looking like a nice hotel lobby. I led Valerie to the receptionist, a late twenty-something dude with a good sun tan, and said, "Here to visit Frances Goldstein, Room 42. My guest is Valerie, um, Fernandez."

"It's Diaz."

"I knew that."

"Okay, buzzing you in," the receptionist dude responded. "Sorry to hear about you and Alexia. I was rooting for you to get the second date."

"Did you bet that I'd get a second date or not?"

"Um, I bet sixty bucks you would not," he told me with a mix of pity and happiness.

"That's great, congrats," I deadpanned.

I felt like a lightning rod, ready to be struck by nerves. I had no idea where Alexia would be but felt suspense to see her because she posted a cute-as-hell selfie of her at the bus stop with the caption: *pray for me, i'm taking the bus in s fla.*

"Can you quit dilly-dallying?" Valerie asked. "I gotta pee really bad,"

"That's insensitive. I'm having a panic attack.."

"Scooch! Where's the nearest bathroom?"

"You have to pee so bad because your laughs of mockery harm the bladder," I told her.

"Whatever."

"Come on, there is a bathroom next to the small TV room, though no one ever uses it, they think the screen is too small."

We walked to the TV room until Valerie left me behind, going into the bathroom. I heard a rerun playing that sounded familiar. I heard more of the dialogue and recognized it was *Sanford and Son.* My dad liked the show cause his dad loved the show about an African American father and son who ran a junk-yard. It was definitely not a show most old Jewish retirees wanted to watch, but it was blasting through the door.

I walked through the fake movie entrance doors to see an old bald man, not Jewish, but the same skin-complexion as Sanford, snoring loudly next to the girl I lost my virginity with, playing with her phone.

Then, Alexia turned around. I felt the past and present merge into a moment you can only see captured in movies where the camera pans around and the feeling of love transcends time and space.

But this wasn't the movies when Alexia said, "Well this would have been more awkward if *Gilmore Girls* were playing."

"I would have lost it like the grumpy dude Luke who runs the diner."

"It's good to see you."

I nearly relented but stood my ground. "It's good to see you too, but just so you know I don't feel any differently. . ."

"Fine," she sighed. "Why are you dressed like that? I hope this wasn't for me, cause it's. . ."

"For your information, I'm up for a job at the corporation called K-Mart. And I assume you're taking the bus home?"

"No, I have a ride. . . we. . . he's picking me up. Going to AA after. That's good you're getting a job, Caldo. Even if you just meet friends or meet another girl. . . like her."

Who knew real pain could be so one-sided?

I turned around and saw Valerie looking like she walked into a spicy telenovela. Yet she was in attack mode, "Um, first no, not going to happen with me, not my type, and you seem to be the type who likes any guy of any age giving you attention. A college girl sleeping with a high school virgin, really? Look at him! This is cruel! You should know better."

"Who the hell are you?"

"I've grown up and enlisted a mentor," I said and then coughed. "We are collaborating on a Shakespeare project."

"Impressive," Alexia said to Valerie. The worst part was she meant it. "You want to get some tea? It's nice to have another girl here. The tea is good! They've got chamomile."

"Sure. I like tea," Valeire said.

"It's good to see you, Caldo," Alexia said. "We'll stay in touch when the time is right. I should schedule a meeting with my sponsor before then about what your friend said." She turned to Valerie. "Thank you for that.

We need sponsors and mentors to do right by ourselves and others."

And then she was gone, and so was Valerie. It was me, a snoring stranger, and Sanford having another heartache mirroring my own.

Act 2: Scene 6

An Elder Doth Dispense Wisdom and Christen a Wingman

The door closed and I started to cry. The snores stopped and a voice said, "All the white folks, old and young, in this place act like they are on a soap opera. This place is one big soap opera. A crying teenager right next to me, like I'm watching a damn play."

Was this old man pretending to sleep to overhear my trauma which was probably more entertaining than *Sanford and Son*?

I felt mortified standing in front of the TV, the son disappointed in Pop. What could I say? All I could do was try my best to stop crying.

"Come on now son, nothing to be embarrassed about. That young white girl is fine as hell, I'd be crying too," the man spoke with wisdom that comes from being too old and tired to bullshit someone. "I was afraid to talk to her cause everyone is so sensitive these days, so I pretended to nap. Now my grandson, that's damn embarrassing, he purposely makes himself look like a fool for money. He paid for this place, not thinking I'd be the only black man in the building. That's the problem of your generation. All the stupid ones are the ones making all the money."

"What does your grandson do?" I asked while reliving Alexia's rejection all over again. At least I was able to hold back the tears.

"He's a popular YouTuber."

"Really, I watch Film YouTube. Who is your grandson?"

"He calls himself Black Logan Paul. Stupid ass name."

A much-needed laugh came out. "I know him, I've seen his prank videos, and he talked about a film I love that no one's ever seen. Kind of a smart name cause he did get a big portion of Logan Paul's audience."

"Nah son, Black Logan Paul is a stupid name, his momma named his dumb ass, Jamal.

"That is pretty cool that your grandson is a successful YouTuber. I once wanted to do stuff with film, he's living the dream."

"You should, any moron with a camera can make white folk money these days."

"Tell that to my mom."

"His grandmother, bless her soul, would be so disappointed, though his momma is proud, but she just likes that he paid her mortgage off. But we are all going through hard times, you're learning about life right now. I lost my Ophelia two years ago and it hurts every day. How long were you with that snowflake? Cause she's fine, not gonna lie. I didn't see you being her type, no offense."

Don't cry. Don't cry, but the tears erupted again and the old man said, "Aw, come on now son. Don't cry, again, it's making us both feel like sloppy joes. Look, we gotta both move on. I found a girl who is annoying as hell and it makes me like her more. Come on, get out yourself a little and be my wing at Bingo."

"Be your wing?" I said through confused tears.

"Yeah, I'm your new friend, Raymond, and I need you to help an old man out by helping me talk to this cute as hell Jewish lady. Never dated one of those, but we are in—different times. Her voice sounds like the redhead on *South Park*, but I like it. Be my wingman, and I'll help you with that Spanish girl."

"I don't like her and she hates me."

"That's how the best relationship begins. Come on, we're both getting back on Cupid's horse."

"I thought Cupid had wings and flew places?"

"That's white people Cupid. Cupid for black people rode a horse and would lasso people into love."

"That's pretty cool."

"See? You're already feeling better. That's the power of Black Cupid. Let's go lasso us some new love."

Act 2: Scene 7

What is Bingo but a Call of the Broken Hearted

Unlike me, the Bingo cage had balls and they were ready to be called.

All eyes were on me and Raymond, the new guy. Really, he the only resident who was a POC. I never saw that many eyes all staring toward me at once. It felt like I could hear their thoughts:

She dumped him after the first date. . .

Way out of his league. . . ...

No way she had sex with that virgin. . .

My eyes drifted toward the back where Alexia and Valerie were actually having tea and looking like they were getting along. There was a snicker shared between the two of them, which I really hope wasn't about me, but in a weird way having Valerie here made this easier. At least it wasn't just me and Alexia staring across the room uncomfortably at each other, reliving the heaven and hell of that night.

"Call Bingo and tell us what happened on the date, Caldo!" an old man called out.

I couldn't find my grandma. Too many people around gawking like they were about to see a show.

Yeah, call Bingo and tell us about the date!"

Alexia and Valerie had matching stares—pity. Valerie put down her tea and walked over.

"I'll be calling Bingo and if anyone wants to ask about my love life they might die," Valerie boomed out and walked up onto the stage. She did have a commanding way about her that probably secured a lot of those debate team victories.

Gratitude entered my body like a guardian spirit to protect me from even more humiliation.

"Come on, help me find my future wife. You can introduce me," Raymond said. "You are like a celebrity here. All they are talking about is you and that Alexia girl. She's gonna think I'm a good guy mentoring you. Make me look good and you'll feel better. Life is about giving."

"If you say so." I snuck a glance at Alexia.

I get why she wanted the space. Hell needed the space. It hurts. It hurts to know she's going to see another guy, and that's what keeps me from truly moving on. Knowing that there is someone else she'd rather spend time with than me. Who was this damn guy? Anger and hurt really do keep you from being a good friend. Until those go away it probably wasn't possible.

"I found her," Raymond gave me a nudge. "I haven't had a crush since I met my first wife, and this old lady is probably gonna be my next one."

Raymond endeared me, open to new love in his widowed years. Maybe one day when I was old and gray, someone could fill the Alexia-shaped hole that'd been left behind.

"I got your back. Whoever she is I will talk you up, Raymond."

"Your generation isn't all bad, or at least you ain't too bad. Alright, follow me. She's close."

I followed him to the back where I saw my grandma sitting with four of her friends. I wondered which friend he was into when my grandma gave me a caring smile and said, "I heard there won't be another date. I'm sorry, Joseph.

"That's your grandma, son? The good Lord works in mysterious ways, this must be a sign."

"Her?" I was kind of stunned.

"I've seen you around, darling. It's good to meet you. I've been mentoring your grandson, he's a good kid. He's like a better version of my own, who's all into movies but makes videos looking like a buffoon."

"This generation is full of buffoons, but Joseph is one exception," she said. "You're a religious man I hear. My late husband was a rabbi. You think God decided we should meet?"

"God gives me blessings, so yes, meeting you is definitely one."

My grandma smiled in a way I hadn't seen her smile in a long time. Valerie placated the crowd with showman-grade Bingo calls, while Alexia was on her phone flirting with the other guy.

Blah. This was my life now.

Act 2: Scene 8

Wherein Lame Doth Finally Pay Off (at K-Mart)

I drove solo to K-Mart not feeling the closure I wanted or maybe even needed. Something from Alexia to make it easier to move on, but she was gone before Bingo ended. It had to be the new guy she got a ride with. Who the hell was he? I hated and envied him. I hated that I felt this way toward a stranger.

Valerie did make the whole ordeal easier. She got a ride home from her mom but said she was never coming back there, and now I had to meet at a library tomorrow to do the Shakespeare project and act less like some Spanish word she used for a dumbass.

I thought of Raymond and Grandma. It was sweet seeing them flirt, a reminder that I am so damn young, yet it feels like adulthood latched onto me when I asked Alexia out on that date. I don't regret it, but I regret the pain and hurt that came with adulthood.

Raymond got my phone number before I left, to help him out in the future and called me his Jewish Hitch. The film snob in me cringed but I politely said the gesture was nice and gave him my number.

The drive felt lonely until I pulled into the K-Mart and the moment felt like another big deal: the first time having sex and a few days later the first time trying to get a job. The K-Mart logo made me think about the future. College. Coding. Film? I parked the car, but it felt like everything was spinning.

I brushed off my khakis and made sure my shirt was tucked in so I wouldn't appear to be too frumpy. I got out of the car and walked toward the store. I could smell the ocean a little bit but it mixed with the mildew and trash on the ground.

I walked into the store and saw a cute cashier with purple hair standing alone, bored. "Hi. I would like to speak to the manager."

"Shit. Why?"

"Oh no, nothing bad. I have an interview."

"Oh right, the new cashier. Hey. I'm Steph."

"Hey, Steph. I'm Caldo."

"Do you party?"

"Occasionally?"

"Cool. It's the only way you get through some days."

"Yeah. So where is the interview?"

"Oh right, it's in the back."

"Thanks."

"Hope you get it."

An old lady came up with ten boxes of cereal.

I went into a back office and saw a large balding man looking at papers with kindergarten-style charts on them. "Joseph Caldo?"

"Yes, sir."

"Good to meet you; I got a high recommendation that you are a good kid who is on the ball, but got dumped and needed to be a man to get a job."

"So you talked to my mom? I see."

The manager rubbed his five o'clock shadow. "Nice lady, your mom. Very persistent. First job. Everyone has to start somewhere, K-Mart is a good place for that. Though I am going to tell you that working at K-Mart might not get you another girlfriend, but it will boost your self-esteem and give you some money, which is as good."

"I could use both of those right now."

"Sure you could, but I have one question cause there is something off with kids your age around here. So if you can answer this question with a no, and I believe you. I'll give you a real chance."

"Great. Ask away."

"Are you on drugs?"

"Oh, no. No way."

"Really?"

"Really. Seriously, you can even test me. I don't do drugs. D.A.R.E. and a Jewish mother made me too paranoid to even try them."

"I can see that talking to her. So you can urinate in a cup and it's going to come out clean?"

"Yes, sir. Totally clean. Finally, being lame is paying off."

"Nothing lame about being drug-free. That garbage is rotting teenage brains. I see it every day. Well, that's good to hear, cause I need cashiers for this time of year. The snowbirds are starting to fly in."

"I'm ready to start as soon as you need me."

"I need people right away. I'll get you on the books and get you trained by Steph this Friday.

"I met her, she's very nice. Great. That works!"

"You don't have a lot of homework or extracurriculars, do you? You'll be doing the night shifts. You get a thirty-minute lunch break."

"Nah. I am not that into school, I don't have any serious or hard homework."

"Between you and me, school is a sham, college too. An honest day of work is what really matters. Friday you'll learn that."

"Great, thank you. I won't let you down." I told him, not knowing if that was true, but feeling something like satisfaction that I finally got my first job.

Act 2: Scene 9

A Most Unfortunate IHOP Reunion

I walked out of K-Mart feeling semi-happy and really hungry. I squinted my eyes, adjusting to the night. I got in my car and felt the need to celebrate. There was only one place to go and that place was IHOP. Sure, I'd fallen down to the hot, lonely hell of South Florida, but I was going to earn a paycheck now. I'd have my own money and maybe that money could be used for, dare I even dream it—film school.

Noticing other girls made me feel excited and alive. This distant dream that had awakened again felt like finding a buried treasure where you could spot a tiny bit of the top sticking out of the quicksand of life.

Yes it was time for pancakes and to get cracked out on mediocre coffee. To take these feelings and maybe think about some kind of film to make sense of them. True inspiration. Maybe Alexia was a muse all along, a way to find my real self. Maybe the old fool Shakespeare was onto something about love being something so transformational that you'd have to write like sixty-nine sonnets or however many he wrote.

I wasn't going to write a sonnet, but maybe I could think of an idea for a short film that didn't totally suck. Maybe I could combine it with the Shakespeare project.

Wow. My first job. For once, I felt like optimism sat in the passenger seat beside me as I parked at the IHOP. I took it inside with me, waving cheerfully at the hostess.

She crunched on a peppermint. "Your friends are back there."

"Friends?" I wondered if she meant my homegirls, a group of escorts who were IHOP regulars and loved me for some reason.

I peered behind the cash register and spotted the back of Alexia's head. That curly-haired bun, I'd recognize it anywhere. Oh shit, she had changed. This was a date? She wasn't alone. The mystery guy was sitting across from her, holding her hand while they sipped coffee.

I wanted to puke, but his dark fuckboy hair that looked familiar peeked above Alexia's bun.

No. God no. My rabbi grandfather told me about Job, and all I could think was that at least Job didn't have Facebook to see his misery reflected back at him.

Then, gasp. My heart quit racing.

Because what. The. Fuck. My bully from freshman year was dating Alexia! The villainous sadistic bastard TONY RIZZIO.

Evil serendipity!

All the hope and momentum I was feeling evaporated when I heard that SoundCloud rapping bastard say, "Waldo Caldo? What are you doing, you little goofy fuck. It's been too long, you little jerk off. Look at you, what are you working at K-Mart now?

I stared down the worst human being I'd ever

known. Rage intertwined with sadness, both flowing through me.

"Tony fucking Rizzio, are you serious?" I said to Alexia's bun like it had the eye of Yahweh.

The same Tony Rizzio who had made freshman year hell. The same guy who had called me Waldo Caldo and made up songs about my supposed small penis. The same guy who had pantsed me in front of the entire cafeteria.

Alexia turned her head around and the chorus from that "I'll Always Love You" song by Whitney Houston shrieked in falsetto from the speakers.

There were coincidences, and then there were moments where you felt like God, the universe, or some bored witch who lived in the Everglades placed a curse on you for fun. This was one of those moments.

"Caldo." Alexia said, startled. "You two know each other?"

My blood turned to gasoline and horrible memories of Tony making my life miserable set it on fire. The awful nicknames he'd given me, the multiple times he'd punched me in the gut and pantsed me in front of the whole high school.

The hostess left me standing there unsure what to do, but Tony got up to shake my hand, "Waldo Caldo. Man, how long has it been, three years? You left school and never returned. You little bitch, I haven't seen you in years. How have you been, you little fuckhead?"

I slapped his hand away. "Him? Really. This is the guy you're dating. You're unsure about me, but him, really?"

"Hey, watch your fucking mouth, Caldo!" Tony barked, standing up a foot away from me, staring me down. "I'll make you feel like you are back in freshman year." He glared at Alexia. "Wait a fucking second. Did I hear this right? You were dating Waldo Caldo?!"

I didn't give a fuck and continued, "And you go here, this is my place, our place, where we had our first date."

"You really dated this little bitch."

"And you bring this stupid-ass loser. This complete total scumbag SoundCloud rapping failure to our—"

A fist flew to my right cheek before I could finish and I fell smack down onto the blue pancake-smelling carpet.

Act 2: Scene 10

Of Love's Final Blow, The Sucker Punch

Before I could get up from the punch and try to defend myself, I heard Alexia scream, "Anthony, go to the fucking car, right now. Go!" She leaned into me. "Caldo, are you okay?"

My pain was put on hold for a second and that *Top Gun* "Take My Breath Away" song started playing. It was like seeing an angel come down to check on me, but then I remembered she was why I felt the pain. Yet I felt no regret for it. This was the person I lost my virginity to, the person who I loved in so many ways.

My jaw throbbed and no words could come out. It felt too real and not real at all, like a dream I would soon wake up from, until Alexia grabbed some ice and put it on my bruised cheek. "Caldo, talk to me, tell me you're okay."

"I'm not okay. I hurt in every possible way now. Every freaking way, but seeing you with him and getting punched by him again. It's the worst pain I've ever felt."

"Again?"

I rubbed my eye. "He bullied me so bad freshman year, it was part of why I am at that stupid school."

"Ah fuck, Caldo. I feel like I am cursing your life. Jesus. I had no idea."

A tear rolled down her cheek as she held my hand. She kept the ice against the bruise below my eye. The chorus blared about breath being taken away. In a weird-ass way, it was a beautiful moment, like I was in some bad *Top Gun* sequel, but this was the moment where she'd finally come back to me. But then I spoke and reality came back. "I love you, Alexia. You're everything I've always looked for. Please tell me there's still hope for you to feel the same."

"There is no hope. I'm sorry. It's not there. I don't feel it, and I'm sober so my feelings are trustworthy. Like I said, I care about you as a friend and hate putting you in pain. We've been over this. This is a friendly reminder. The key word being friendly."

"But you like that fucking asshole over me?" I asked masochistically.

"He's just a guy, Caldo. He's here to alleviate the loneliness I can't drink away."

I understood right there and then that we were the same, but we were in different places. She was an adult, and I definitely was not. She needed to find a guy who was, but it pained me that the best she could do was fucking Tony Rizzio.

"I understand," I shared my thoughts. "Then promise me something. Promise me that you'll find someone who makes you feel the way you make me feel."

"I'll make that promise under one condition. You have to promise me you'll do something with film again.

Otherwise, you run the risk of becoming a snooze-fest person and I won't stand for it."

"It's a wound I'm not sure I'm ready to take the Band-Aid off yet," I said. "I will work on it."

"Deal. I'll work on my end of the bargain, too. Once we are ready to commit to these things, that's when we'll be friends again. I promise."

Act 2: Scene 11

Shakespeare Probably Needed Therapy (That'seth a Loteth)

My mom took one look at my shiner and threw a fit. She forced me to stay home and said I looked run-down and didn't want me getting sick for the job I'd start on Friday. I lied and said it was a drunk guy at IHOP, knowing that if I told her it was an old bully who was now dating Alexia she would have pressed charges, and that is the only way Tony's SoundCloud rap career would go anywhere.

She had me still do my appointment with Heller, but now it would be on the phone.

"Hello, Joseph. Sorry I can't see you in person. Your mom said you got accosted and are very injured. Are you okay?"

"I got punched in the face and it's the least painful thing that happened, Dr. Heller. I'm fine, it's nice to take time off from school. Although I am going to sneak out to the library today. I got a mentor and a job, I'm like a fucking adult now."

"Let's start with the pain, though I'm intrigued by

the idea of you going to a library and a job that's a surprise."

"Here's a bigger surprise: I had sex with Alexia. We had sex. Good sex. Nice sex. Really special kind of sex that old white guys write boring poems about."

"Woah. . . " Dr. Heller said not in shrink tone.

"Woah indeed, I lost my virginity to pretty much the best friend that I had fallen in love with, who saw this as a hookup, and the pain of that outweighs the pleasure of the sex, which most guys would say is insane, but I am talking to a shrink right now so who knows."

"Well. . . that's a lot."

"Do you think coincidences are cruel jokes by God?"

. . .

"Paging Dr. Heller."

"I am not sure God played a role, but that is unfortunate."

"Nothing is fair in love and war, just like Shakespeare said."

"I'm no Pulitzer Prize winner, Joseph, but I don't think that's the quote nor the author."

"Whatever. That guy depresses the fuck out of me. Can you up my meds?"

"Ha. No. I think we are on a good dose of Effexor, which unfortunately won't fix teen angst. You mentioned a job, and a mentor who you are meeting at the library. I am frankly in awe of your progress toward adulthood, even though you pretend to be hiding from it."

"You got a point there. My mom gave me an ultimatum and now I am going to work at K-Mart and the school has this new girl to help me be less of a fuck up.

She came with me to the nursing home yesterday cause I didn't want to see Alexia on my own."

"That's nice of her. She's maybe a friend or something even more?"

"No way. She's too annoying. Way more annoying than my mom and somehow more critical. No thanks." My phone rang. It was my grandma's nursing home. "I need to take this."

"I understand."

I expected to hear a nurse delivering the worst news imaginable, but it was Raymond. "Joseph Caldo, my man, tell me where I should take your grandma to dinner. Where do Jewish women like to eat at? I learned they don't do ribs."

"Raymond, I thought something bad happened."

"Yeah, I learned I can't take Jewish women to get ribs. That's pretty bad. I knew the best rib spot in town. Where am I going to take your grandma now?"

"Ah man, you gotta take her to the Cheesecake Factory. She loves that place."

"Is that where you took your girl?"

"No, I took her to IHOP."

"You messed up son, should have took her to the Cheesecake Factory, and if you get a date with the nice Spanish girl you better not take her to no IHOP."

"I'm taking her to the library and that's about it."

"That is where you take the good girl's son."

My phone buzzed again. I was running a hotline that day. A text from an unknown number: *Stay away from Alexia or next time will be worse.*

toNy

PTSD quaked through my bones. I wished I had an outlet besides Dr. Heller, who increasingly didn't know what to make of me.

Act 2: Scene 12

It felt so weird to sneak out to go to the library. We could have met by the school but Valerie said she wasn't able to think well with Charles lurking around. We met at the West Boca Raton library, which looked more like a DMV than a place to study.

She was dressed in baggy sweatpants and a light sweater for the University of Central Florida. It was the kind of outfit that said to me: I truly do not see you as a romantic option. It shouldn't have bothered me but did anyway.

"What happened to your face? Jesus. Who punched you?"

"Alexia's new boyfriend. My old bully from high school. Awesome blossom, right?"

She started laughing but stopped when it occurred to her I might be serious. "Oh damn. . ."

"Yeah, you two got along yesterday." I held open the door for her to enter the library.

"I gotta be honest Caldo, I am kind of impressed she

hooked up with you. She's very hot and cool. Like, I didn't think you could pull that off. A college girl too, it reminds me that I should shoot for my own dream colleges."

"Are you saying that me having sex with Alexia is like you trying to get into Harvard?" I shot back in a high-pitched voice.

"Shh. . ." Valerie said, directing me to the front desk. "We are in the library, respect the rules."

We arrived at the desk and a woman with short hair and big glasses smiled. "Valerie, good to see you. Tutoring session?"

"Hi Donna, yes definitely tutoring. Could we have the room with the plays? I'm trying to inspire this. . . young man?"

"If you think it'll work. You'd be surprised how rarely paintings of the great playwrights spark inspiration in the greater public."

"It's because we are philistines who like movies and music because they are better," I piped in. "Not my fault."

I followed Valerie down a hallway of tiny rooms which annoyed me because they resembled our stupid school. "So did I miss anything important today?"

"Not really, though I informed Fane and Charles you definitely did sleep with a hot college girl. They might bully you less or maybe more out of jealousy."

"So what did you and Alexia talk about?"

"We talked about girl stuff, not about you, if you must know."

"Nothing about me?"

"We talked about what to major in college, which is what we need to talk about besides the project, and what guys are good to date. She did say you're a good guy, and I learned she is a little crazy when she said I should date you."

"She said that?"

"Yeah, she did. I said you weren't my type at all, and she said she thought that too. But then she said to make sure you do film and that I be a good friend to you. It was sweet and sad. She does care about you. She just knows. . ."

"I know."

"Maybe we can put this into the Shakespeare project. Instead of doing something generic about *Romeo and Juliet*, what if we focused on the idea of unrequited love? There's this whole theme in his work about people who love someone who doesn't love them back."

"Have you experienced that too?"

"Maybe. But that's personal and we barely know each other."

"Come on, that's not fair, you literally bonded with the person who took my virginity."

"Fine. All I'll say is the person who took my virginity also broke me. You're not special, if it's any consolation."

I appreciated her sharing that and it helped me understand who Valerie was. Why she was guarded, focused on school, focused on things she could control, and I probably drove her a little nuts by having her life tied to mine kind of unfairly. "We'll do something good for Connie. I'm hesitant to do film but that's probably what we should do for this. Either way I'm already sick and tired of thinking about unrequited love."

"Fair enough, we'll figure something out. I always wanted to do something with film. It would be cool, it would look good on college applications, they love creative stuff."

I nodded. Valerie was so good at adulthood. So good at everything. I kind of admired her, and though she was guarded she seemed to have the answers about everything outside of love.

"I'm starting a job and might use that money to save for film school, just don't tell my mother or anyone else this. Any pointers on how to not get fired and be better at school?"

"Do the job that's assigned and study. If you don't bomb this assignment, you'll be fine. You're smarter than you act, that I can tell, but you are like so many guys—you will do something self-destructive and dumb over a girl."

Act 3

Act 3: Scene 1

Our Hero Doth Embrace a Fair Bieber

When Friday came around for my first day at K-Mart I did feel a little better. A little more focused and refreshed. I even wanted to do a little better in school. I wasn't like a new man or anything. I just didn't feel as bad as I had last Friday night after the virginity-sex-loss of best friend debacle.

As the sun went down I drove and drove until I saw the K-Mart sign. I made the turn into the parking lot and I felt déjà vu, but not in the soul-crushing way that I usually experienced in South Florida. I felt weirdly excited to start my first job.

I parked near the K-Mart entrance and got out of the car. I checked myself out in the dimly lit car reflection. I looked super lame in this uniform, but at least I'd get paid for it. I walked past the dying street lamps and headed on through the dingy doors. Fingerprints smeared in a halo so bright I had to squint my eyes.

It wasn't too busy except for a few people browsing around the out-of-season holiday clearances. I passed the cashiers and went past the women's clothes to the manager's room. I made it past the exit door and saw my boss in his office talking on the phone. He held his index finger up at me to give him a second.

I stood by the door until he put the phone down. "You look sharp, Caldo. I'm feeling a little better about you. You passed your piss test and you're early." He got up from his desk and stretched. "Follow me. You're getting trained under Steph."

I followed him out of the office and we walked to the cash registers up front. He pointed to them and I saw him focusing on the cute girl I'd met before with crazy-looking rainbow hair. She didn't notice us and focused on getting the customer's order. "Steph acts like a damn hippie, but she's got impressive register time. Watch her. Ask questions. Stay out of trouble. No peanut gallery remarks or rudeness. Ignore her kooky hair and be respectful. Got it?"

"Got it."

We walked over to Steph. Her rainbow hair made me feel a little dizzy, but she seemed so bright and happy. I didn't know how she beamed positivity while working at K-Mart, but she was making it work.

The manager gestured toward her like he was rolling out a red carpet. "Alright, Steph. You're our leading lady. Show him the ropes. Let him watch and then help him manage the register. Got it?"

"Got it, boss. I'll school him right."

"Good. Loving the positivity. I'm going to check on the toy section. Lots of people doing weird stuff over there. Sickos—doing weird stuff to those old Justin Bieber dolls that should be in the landfill. They must be cursed or something."

"I liked him when I was younger."

"Figures. Alright, train Caldo while I handle the old Biebs merch."

He walked to the entertainment section, leaving me and Steph. Then, the terrible impulse rose. The one I'd tried to shut down—the desire to have sex again. Why couldn't I have no sexuality, like a starfish?

Damn, I didn't realize having sex with Alexia would make interacting with other girls harder. None of this adult/sex stuff made sense.

She kept smiling at me. I tried to change the vibe, "Thanks for helping me."

"It's my job, dude. It's all good. I got you."

"Thanks."

"Nah, dude Thank you," she said with a Joker-like expression.

I was beginning to wonder what Steph's deal was. She was weird, like weird in that way the kids at my school were weird.

She gave me a playful punch. "Hey man, relax. There isn't anything to be nervous about. This job is super easy. Chillax. I'll help with your nerves after break. I got my tricks. As long as you know basic math and know how to scan stuff, you can totally do this job high. Watch."

An old man by himself with no cart approached us. He dropped a container of Metamucil and a magazine about guns on the conveyor belt. "Your hair looks like a leprechaun took a piss on it. It hurts my eyes."

She beamed. "I love leprechauns. They're so cool. Is that debit or credit?"

"Neither. Cash."

She bagged his stuff and handed him back his change then he speed-walked out.

"Old dudes. So honest. We're all so afraid to share what we really feel."

I was starting to sense there was something not quite right about Steph. Would I never find normal friends? Hell, would I ever even be normal myself?

The line was now empty and she looked away from the register and stared into my eyes. "Joseph, I sense a sadness about you. I know I just met you, but I can sense people's spirits and you have a beautiful spirit. I can taste it. It's like gummy bear vitamins."

She rubbed my arm. "I take those daily. I take the Vitamin D ones. Thanks."

I liked the feeling of being touched. Her arms were strong but delicate and felt nice against mine. She let my hand go and took a big gulp from her water bottle. "Let's go on break now."

"But we just started."

"It's fine, dude. It's dead right now. A small break."

"Okay. You know what's best."

"I do. I want to show you something special. Something to make you the gummy bear vitamin you were born to be."

We walked out the front door and circled around to the back of the store. There was no one there, only trash bags and cigarette butts. She lit a cigarette. "Do you feel the wind? It feels like ghost fingers. I bet it's the ghost souls who were once masseuses in ancient Mesopotamia."

I truly did not know what she meant and I wondered why she wasn't at my school. "I truly did not know what she meant but offered up my own expertise. "I can't speak on the ghosts of Mesopotamia, but as a child I liked *Ghost Hunters* and was very against the Iraq war. That's the same region, right?"

"I like how your brain works."

"I'm glad somebody does."

"Your brain needs to be like my brain now. Then it would be the best brain."

"Are you on drugs?"

"Duh."

Everything made sense now. Most kids over fifteen in South Florida were on some type of drug.

"Are you going to arrest me, officer?"

"No."

She rubbed my chest. "Although I believe in fuck the police, I gotta say you'd be kind of hot as a cop. It would balance you out. Yin and yang. You should do some Molly, too. It'll help with the training."

She kept rubbing my chest which weirded me out, but I felt myself getting hard and the good parts of my brain stopped working, or maybe it was working how a seventeen-year-old horny boy's brain was programmed to work?

She stopped rubbing. "I've never really done drugs. I'm on meds and stuff. I'm not supposed to do anything. It could mess with the meds."

"That's stupid. Molly is soul medication," she put her cigarette out and then started rubbing my arms, but it wasn't sexual. It felt like she was doing it because I was there, but my boner didn't care and I felt myself being pushed into doing something that was probably going to be really dumb. I tried to hold onto what Valerie said a few days ago about not doing dumb things cause of girls, but her voice dissolved the more Steph touched me.

She kept rubbing my arm. "You're really cute. You're heavy on the yin but I can feel the yang in you too."

"Thanks."

"This will make you at one with me and the wind, so we'll truly know each other."

I stared at the harmless looking pill.

"I can see your chakras are closed. This will open them. This will stop all that pain."

"My shrink said that the Effexor and Adderall can react strangely with certain drugs, so I gotta be careful."

"This isn't a drug, man. It's a portal. Come on, I don't want to roll alone. When I saw you I thought you'd be cool." She held my hands and locked her eyes into mine. "I want to do this with you."

"My mom told me that Dr. Phil said Ecstasy causes your bones to melt. I don't want my bones to melt."

"Your mom and Dr. Phil are fucking dumb, man."

"That's the truest statement I've heard in a long time."

I'd barely been living. For better or worse I'd done things in the past week I never thought possible. Crazy impossible things. What was one more nutty thing going to really do to me? This job kind of sucked, it would be better if I was high.

I shrugged and said, "Alright, YOLO."

"YES! Put out your tongue and trust me." She placed a little blue circle on my tongue. I swallowed it down. "Hold out your tongue again. I need proof."

"When does it start to work?"

She put her tongue on top of mine in a sudden makeout moment. It was messy but it felt really good. There was no connection like I'd had with Alexia, but my body didn't seem to care. We continued to kiss until she abruptly ripped her head away and wiped my saliva from her chin. Let's take another break in an hour."

I felt a pep in my step.

I followed her back inside to the cash register. The setting made things feel normal again, but as time passed I started to feel really thirsty and really different.

I leaned behind the cash register, chugging a bunch of water from the bottle Steph and I had been sharing. I was so thirsty, but I felt so good. I felt so good about everything, and I liked how the conveyor belt felt against my hands. I liked how Steph's hair felt when it brushed against my neck while she explained what the buttons did. I liked how the buttons felt, I liked how everything felt. Even when the Boomers gave me dirty looks.

This job wasn't so bad, minutes were flying by but they felt like happy drops in a pond. Could minutes really fly?

I was forgetting about Alexia and the future, and was enjoying my new friend Steph.

I handed her the big water bottle. "I like you. You're like Rainbow Brite and Prozac had a cool baby. I hope you marry GI Joe, because you deserve an American hero. Steph, you're my hero. Your hair is its own flag."

"Oh, thanks dude. You too. You need to know you're your own country. You need to salute yourself."

"I don't know what that means, but thanks." The manager was coming over, but man, he looked like a bear and I wanted to hug him. Steph, I know I can't hug the boss but the urge is strong. He looks like a teddy bear in the woods."

"Man. We gotta calm down. Get centered. Find your third eye chakra and act normie as fuck. Be quiet and only say yes or no to anything. Nothing else. He can't know that you're rolling. I'm a pro at it. Act like a robot and you'll be good."

"Okay. I can do that. I can be that."

The manager joined us by Steph's register. "You getting the hang of this, Caldo?"

"Yes, sir, it's been great. I love this job."

"You don't have to BS me, Caldo. Though this is a good starter job for a kid. But now I want you to make yourself useful."

"I want to be of use. I'm here for that."

"No crap, that's why I hired you. This is what you're going to do. Go to the toy section and clean up and organize. The toys are all over the place. Go fix it, Caldo."

"Yes, sir. I shall go."

"Of course you will, I told you to."

"I love toys. They're great. I'm going right now."

He frowned at me and walked away.

Steph twirled her hair. "Bye, Rainbow Brite. I shall go to the toys for I am but a toy of K-Mart."

"Give them hugs and love."

I meandered off, cutting through the women's garment section. I liked how the dresses felt against my arms. They felt like cool caterpillars.

I passed through to the jeans and t-shirt section and a charming old couple came up to me. The woman asked, "Excuse me, son, where are the video games? We want to get a gift for our grandson."

"Listen. These video games, they aren't real. Your grandson wants a connection and for you to really know him, and the only way you can do that is by knitting him a sweater so he stays warm. Wow, it's really hot in here."

"Sonny, we're in Florida. He doesn't need a sweater."

The old woman smiled. "We want to get him one of those racing games."

"No. Give him something real. Drive him in a real car to a real race."

"Let's go to the electronics section, Darlene," the old man said.

I left the old people and walked toward the toys. They looked so happy, especially the Care Bears, sitting there by themselves. I got closer to the toys and saw two bears staring at one another. "You two belong together," I told them. "If there are toy salmons I shall put them in your mouths and let you eat. Natural selection. What a tragic thing. Tragic but true."

A little boy looking at the coloring books looked scared. His mom was behind him, and he said to her, "Mommy, I don't want to play with toys anymore. Can we please go home?"

I knew I was supposed to be doing something in the toy section, but I kept looking at Malibu Barbie and brushing her hair with my pinky nail. "You're so pretty. I knew a pretty girl like you, but she's with Skeletor now. Seriously, Tony Rizzio looks like a Pisan Skeletor. Girls like Alexia think that's hot. Hopefully, like you, she'll find Ken. I wish I was Ken for like two more weeks. Alexia would have at least dated me a little longer. I miss her, but I get that we're supposed to be super friends. I'm not her Ken. Lucky, Ken. Are there only Kens in your universe, Barbie?"

I meditated on that deep question and put Barbie down as the K-Mart radio millennial pop hit station changed to that song Justin Bieber wrote about babies. The aisle was a graveyard of Bieber dolls rotting on the ground. Old and withered from being on the shelf too long. No one had come to deliver prayers and flowers. They deserved better.

Then, a message from the void: I, Caldo, was the

chosen one. The gods had called upon me to elevate their frequencies.

I picked up the cleanest one. "Hey, Justin. Don't worry. You're still singing from the sky. You used to be so nice. What happened with Selena? An underrated actress. We messed up. We lost the best women."

I held the Justin doll up and hugged him. "We're going to get through this. We're going to be alright." I hugged him so hard, like I wanted to be hugged, and then started dancing with him. I slow-danced with him to his song and I could feel a family watching me and hear their children laughing. Children had such joyous laughter.

The laughter and joy only grew while I held Bieber in my arms. "I know you moved on from Selena and got married, and that's beautiful. That gives me so much strength right now. Please keep singing to me. I want to be comforted by your truth, Biebs." I held the Justin Bieber doll tighter and told him, "I'm going to move on, Justin. Alexia is going to be happy and I will find love again. It's not Rainbow Brite, though I would definitely hook up with her. But deep down, my dude, I want to feel love and I want to give love. People loved your songs and they all suck. If I made films and they sucked, would people still love them? Maybe they would? Maybe fear isn't really real."

I felt a wave of exhaustion hit me as I lay down with Bieber. I felt like we needed more love, so I grabbed SpongeBob SquarePants and we all did a group cuddle. "Dudes, it's so nice to meet other guys who really get me. Even though you're dolls, you guys are real. We're young men who search from land to sea to find love again."

I held both of them tighter and felt joy, but then I

heard an angry voice, "What in God's name are you freaking doing to those dolls, Caldo!?"

Families witnessed this event in the modern way, taking pictures and videos with their phones. The boss held up his hands in protest, and I heard him tell them, "Folks, please don't take any video recordings. We hire special people here and sometimes it can go a little awry. Caldo, put down the SpongeBob and Justin Bieber dolls and get in my office right now!"

Act 3: Scene 2

The Villainous Market Manager Hath Scorned Me

I sat in my boss' office staring at the strand of blond hair from the Justin Bieber doll that was stuck in my pinky fingernail.

"Caldo, snap out of it!" His nostrils flared with each breath like a cartoon bull about to charge. The fluorescent lights above us buzzed with the intensity of a thousand judgy bees.

"May I please have some water?"

"You know how long I have worked in K-Mart and managed this place?"

"A long time. You're a nice man and you do a good job." I added with absolute conviction, "Your blue vest really brings out your eyes. Has anyone ever told you that you look like a majestic, hairless Mufasa?"

He rolled a bottle of water across the table so he wouldn't have to come close to me. "Drink it and shut the hell up. This is what I get for doing favors for people."

I drank the whole thing down and let out a burp that echoed in the tiny office like Chewbacca's mating call. For a second, I was convinced I could see the sound waves rippling through the air. I was feeling less touchy and a little bit more grounded in reality; it was starting to hit me that spooning Justin Bieber and SpongeBob SquarePants dolls was probably not a good thing to do on my first day.

I threw the water away. "I think somebody drugged me. I still feel the drug in my system. It's the Ecstasy. The kids call her Molly."

"Bullshit. This is the last time I hire somebody who has a couple of screws loose." He gestured at a security monitor on his desk. "The cameras caught everything. You told SpongeBob you were his pineapple under the sea. You asked Justin Bieber if his hair was made of angel feathers and then tried to smell it to confirm your theory!"

"I'm not crazy."

"You did stuff to the dolls, son. Justin Bieber and poor SpongeBob! The employees in electronics are calling you Toy Story XXX! You need help. I hope the corporation doesn't have this place bugged, but it's pretty sad when I can't even say you're K-Mart cashier material."

"Oh man, please don't fire me. I need a job. Take pity on me."

"Oh, I have pity, son. I pity your family. They're good people and I feel bad for them. They're gonna see you on YouTube now, doing sex stuff to a Justin Bieber doll."

"It wasn't sex stuff!" I protested, though my drug-addled brain helpfully replayed footage of me tenderly caressing Bieber's plastic cheek and whispering, "Your voice is like hot caramel on my eardrums."

"Whatever it was, it wasn't right!"

"So I'm definitely fired?"

"Yeah. Hello! You're lucky I don't report you to the police for doing sex stuff to dolls in front of minors."

"No! Please don't, sir." A vivid image flashed in my head of a future where I'd have to introduce myself to new neighbors: "Hi, I'm Joseph, and I'm legally required to tell you I'm on a registry. . . for inappropriate relations with a Canadian pop star action figure."

He sucked in his spit, disgusted. "I'm not. It wouldn't be fair to your family. It's bad enough they have had to raise you. Right now, I want someone to come pick you up and take you off my hands. You're three sheets to the wind. I can't let you go home like that, so you better get a ride or I'm gonna have the police come and get you."

"Man. I don't have any friends."

"That might be the least surprising thing you've said today. You better call your poor mother before I do."

I was screwed. Mom would murder me. Dad would be disappointed but understanding. But there was one other option—the person who was supposed to be helping me not completely destroy my life.

I swallowed my pride and pressed her number. Four rings went by and I heard her pick up.

"Hey, Valerie. I think I need your mentorship again, like right now."

Act 3: Scene 3

Valentina Doth Send an Escape Horse (Pulls Up in a Jeep)

Twenty-three minutes later, I was somewhat sober when Valerie walked into the K-Mart office. Her hair was in a bun, and she was wearing sweatpants and an oversized white t-shirt.

She looked at me like I was a piece of furniture that had unexpectedly caught fire. "I'm here to pick up this fool."

"You appear to be a decent and intelligent young woman. What are you doing befriending this deviant?"

"We go to school together. Our teacher suggested I mentor him, but it turns out I'm also his keeper."

"Sorry to hear. I hope you get college credit for it."

"Ya think?"

"Very well, then. Get him the hell out of here. And you're banned from this store, Caldo. You're banned."

"What if I need to buy deodorant?"

"You can do so at the Publix."

I followed Valerie, feeling like a little kid leaving the principal's office with his mom.

As we made our way toward the cash register I said,

"Wait, I gotta say goodbye to Steph. Try to get her number or something."

"Are you serious? How about, 'Thank you, Valerie, for picking me up on a Friday night after I got fired from my job for doing drugs and acting like a damn tonto.' Literally, I said like five seconds ago to cut it out with the stupid shit and grow up."

"Thank you, Valerie, for picking me up on a Friday night and the rest of the stuff you said including the t-word."

"She drugged you! Get the fuck out of here. We're going."

I ignored Valerie and approached Steph. "Hey, it was a lot of fun hanging with you. We should hang out again. Like, give me your number and stuff."

Steph looked at Valerie. "You're very pretty. Like in an Ugly Betty kind of way."

I waved my hands. "Hello? Did you hear me? Let's exchange digits."

"Nah."

"Nah?"

"You heard it. Nah. You do stuff with dolls. Furries aren't my thing, man," she said. She caught the boss man inspecting her. "Please leave. I don't talk to drug users."

The boss pointed at the exit. "Didn't you hear the girl? Get out of here!"

Valerie and I walked out, got inside her blue Jeep, and sat in a never-ending silence before she barked, "Do you need help putting your seatbelt on, or what?"

I focused with all my energy and put my seatbelt on. "Sorry, I'm still in a haze and I think I did weird stuff with dolls."

She burst out laughing. "Please tell me what

happened with the dolls. What did you do with the dolls?"

"It isn't funny. I can barely speak. I need food. Gotta get my HP up."

"If you're paying. I'm hungry too. Mom and I get dinner every Friday because she works the night shifts at the hospital. It's like our only time together."

The guilt sobered me right up. "I'm sorry. It was an emergency."

"I hope no one's there. I can't be seen in public with the K-Mart doll diddler," she said.

"God, I hope this isn't already up on YouTube."

Her stomach growled. "What are we eating?"

"I'm an IHOP kinda guy. I need bacon and a coffee with cream that comes out of one of those tiny silver pitchers." She smirked. "What's so funny?" I asked.

"Life. My ex would take me to The Cheesecake Factory, and now I'm going with the K-Mart doll diddler to IHOP. God, high school keeps getting worse. I can't wait for college."

Act 3: Scene 4

Thou Deathest Approaches Robed in Bullshit

Even the blue and white light of the IHOP logo frowned upon us. "Let's get this over with. I'm starving," declared Valerie.

As the Ecstasy wore off, I faded from a warm caterpillar into a cold centipede. Somehow, I was grateful for Valerie's scorn. Glad I wasn't with my mother.

The host nodded with approval. "New girlfriend? Wow. That was fast," she exclaimed and winked.

Valerie wagged a finger. "Oh no. No, no-no-no-no."

"Yikes," the host replied. "It's good to see you making friends. This one seems to hate you, but your other ones are here, too. No funny business though. Another food fight and everyone is banned."

"I understand. Thanks, Donna."

She escorted us to our table and Valerie whisper-asked, "How often do you come here? And what food fight?"

Before I could answer, I saw my homegirl sex workers sitting in the back eating pancakes.

Rivera held up her fist and pounded her heart. "Mr.

Caldo with a fine-looking Latina. Hola, hermosita! Come over and meet Caldo's honorary older sister."

"I come here a decent amount," I said.

"Honorary older sister?" Valerie asked.

"Let's go and say hi. I'll explain later."

"Caldo, look at you looking all cute with your new girl. Give me a hug," Rivera said, her arms open.

We hugged and the other girls checked out Valerie. She was standoffish. "Mi novio? Noooo. No es mi novio! I'm Valerie. I'm Caldo's mentor for school."

"Girl, you know your name is Valentina."

"The white kids in the gifted program all call me Valerie. Supongo que se quedó."

"Sí, I understand. I was in the gifted program, too," Rivera said. "Well alright, Valerie. So you're Caldo's tutor. I love to see a Latina leading lost white boys for once. I love to see it. But Caldo's a good kid. A while back, I did some English homework on *Madame Bovary* with your boy. You read it?"

"For AP English. *Madame Bovary* is one of my favorite books. You liked *Madame Bovary*, Caldo?"

"Yeah, I mean you could say it's about a girl who poisoned herself just for shopping and getting too much D." Valerie shot me a look of horror, but I continued, "But it's really about the struggle to want it all when you can never have it all, and how do you choose to live realizing that shitty truth. Her poisoning herself and banging that guy was her choosing to live. Like Flaubert said, c'est moi. I related to the book."

No one replied but I was on fire and added, "I want to do a retelling of it, but have it be a transwoman shot like a *Real Housewives* episode—all that drama but with actual depth." Boom. Mic drop.

Rivera and her crew started clapping. "Girl, I set

him up for you. So what's up, you want to be a literature teacher or something?"

Valerie nodded with pride. "Yeah. PhD. Todo el asunto."

"We love to see it. Latinas being their best selves," Rivera said with pride and held up her fist to give her a pound.

"Sí, definitivamente."

There was real joy in Rivera's eyes. When she'd met Alexia she was impressed with her hotness, but with Valerie it seemed like she was impressed with who she was. "Girl, it's such a pleasure to meet you. Mucho amor y respeto. And always good to see you, Caldo. She's a good one. Follow her lead and you'll be fine."

Rivera and her friends went back to their table and Valerie and I went back to ours.

Valerie sat down and took a long, deep breath. "This isn't how I expected to spend my night, but those girls are cool." Now that we were alone again, it was high time for more scolding. If she weren't across the table, she'd grab onto my ear. "I can't believe you, Caldo. Who tries Ecstasy on their first day at a job? Dios mío, man."

"I thought me and Rainbow Brite were gonna, you know, after work."

"Why are guys so dumb when it comes to sex?"

"I don't know. Why are girls not?"

"We are dumb, trust me. We just save all that stupidity for one person."

Our food came and we dug into our pancakes. They tasted so good, and Valerie didn't hold back until she let out a little belch.

"Whoops. Sorry."

I kept eating. "It's IHOP. If you don't burp you've ordered the wrong food."

"My ex made a huge deal that I burped in front of his friends."

"Lame."

"He was all healthy, too. My Mom is uber-healthy. She's into the whole gluten-free keto stuff. It drives me crazy."

"This is why I come here. Mom makes me eat ridiculously healthy, too. I didn't know Puerto Rican moms were as neurotic as Jewish ones."

"All moms are neurotic after they've lived in South Florida for a few years. But damn, Caldo. You're pretty screwed. My ma would make me wish for death if I did what you did."

I put my head on the table like it would hide me from everything. The little spark and hope of maybe going to college to study film felt hopeless without a job. My parents would only help and pay for me to do tech/code stuff, and it was too late for me to get any kind of scholarship. I wished I knew film people, but all I'd done was furiously insert myself into the discourse on film forums, which pissed most people off.

"Come on, sit up, Caldo. Don't be a baby, you did something super stupid over a girl, so has every other guy in existence. You can get another job."

"Who is going to hire me now? I'm going to be the Bieber Diddler of Boca Raton, no employer wants that!" She started laughing hysterically into her pancakes and I protested, "This isn't funny, come on."

"You'll be fine, you're a privileged white guy, you'll bounce back."

"I'm not made of rubber or whatever. I don't bounce. I wallow, which is a privileged white guy thing to do, I suppose. How do you push forward, not fuck up, and be perfect?"

She sipped the coffee. "I'm not perfect, but I have to be close to it. I'm a young Puerto Rican woman who wants to be a professor and write about English literature. I don't have the privilege of not being excellent. I gotta be like this if I want to even have a shot. I want to be the first woman in my family to go to college. You keep mentioning film, are you gonna grow some cojones and go to film school? What's the plan?"

My throat felt dry again. The anxiety of following through was there, yet somehow Valerie seeing me at my worst and not totally shunning me helped me feel like I could open up.

"Okay. So yes, I'd like to make films. I'd like to meet people who have made films and learn to make them. I'd be happy to even make commercials. Start somewhere and go from there. I used to love being behind a camera. It was my happy place, finding ways to capture life through it. I could see so much behind a lens. But I stopped."

"Why?"

"Something really bad happened when I was filming and Mom made me quit, and I never picked it up again. I couldn't even film now even if I wanted to, but I want to, but can't seem to do it. . . it's complicated."

"Damn, Caldo. You should like, talk to a shrink."

"I do. I never really bring it up. I don't like to talk about personal stuff. Unless it's about being in love with a college girl."

"You're a mess, Caldo. Jesus. But I feel you. I don't like sharing certain personal stuff either. It's like the one thing we have in common."

"You've let a few things slip about stuff about your ex. I'm so curious about what this guy was like."

"Some guy. Some cliché that every girl wants. The high school quarterback. Tall. Easy on the eyes. Girls love him. Guys want to be him. A guy who has everything, so a girlfriend who loves him isn't enough! Basically the opposite of you. Except he wasn't that funny and you're also not that funny." She paused and gave her don't-be-so-sensitive-Caldo look. "You're not a lost cause. You have some semi-redeemable qualities."

"I don't know. I feel screwed. I don't know who the hell would hire me or if I'll ever even live to see the day once Mom gets her hands on me."

"If she gets to you before we finish this project, I'll be so pissed at her."

I fiddled with my hands. "I appreciate you helping me out, but film school doesn't care much about grades. I gotta figure out some way to make money and save up for a camera instead of worrying about that school bullshit."

"What if I could get you another job? Like right away? Like maybe even tomorrow?"

"Woah. Really? Wait. Is this some multi-level marketing thing? Cause I'm not suave enough to be a racketeer."

"No, Caldo. A real job with a pay stub and solid pay."

"This isn't a trick?"

"No lie. But! On the condition you pay attention to our Shakespeare project. Which you should have been doing already. Like by yesterday. We wasted a whole library day."

I squinted. "Feels too good to be true."

"It's not. I have a cousin who manages an. . . established. . . well respected. . . eatery. He needs somebody for nights and weekends. I can text him if you're up for the challenge."

"What are the requirements for the English project again?"

"Oh-em-ef-gee. We have to show Shakespeare is pertinent to our own lives using a creative art form."

"Deal."

I held my hand out and she shook it. She whipped out her phone and texted at lightning speed.

Ding.

She must have been President Obama getting an answer that fast.

"All set up. Your interview is tomorrow."

"But what is the job?" No response. "Ma'am?"

"Congrats on being the new Chuck E. Cheese mouse of Lantana, Florida."

Act 3: Scene 5

Wherein Dreams Turn to Memes Most Foul

I paid for the meal and followed Valerie to her car. The knowledge of probably being the next Chuck E. Cheese had sobered me up completely. She got onto the highway and put my address into the phone's GPS.

"So should I call you Caldo, Chuck E. or Chuck E. Cheese Caldo?" she joked.

"You're such an asshole."

One of the things I missed the most about Alexia was cruising around the lamest places in South Florida. But this felt different—less desperate, more real.

Valerie made a left and seemed to be caught up in her thoughts as well. I wondered if she missed driving around with someone too. I couldn't believe she'd dated the high school quarterback. She didn't seem like the type who'd be into quarterbacks, but this guy probably was a blockbuster.

"Do you miss your ex on Friday nights?" I asked.

"Well, do you miss Alexia tonight?" she asked, annoyed.

"Fine, I won't go there. I do miss her. You negging me makes me miss that a lot."

"Brad was way nicer and even sweet when we were alone in his car. His car was pretty baller too."

My lame-ass car was still parked at K-Mart. I'd need a ride tomorrow, which meant I'd have to tell my mom. Ugh. If she hadn't heard already. I didn't want to deal with this today. I was out of fuel. So instead, I asked, "Did you feel famous being the QB's girlfriend?"

She didn't answer and flipped a question on me like a defense lawyer. "Do you miss being at a regular school?"

"I didn't until now, when I'm realizing how isolated I've been. The bullies are worse in regular school. But maybe being lonely is worse."

Valerie kept driving but I saw her steal a little glance at me. This time, empathy instead of pity. "Damn, Caldo. You've been at this crazy school for a while. That must be hard. I've been there for less than a week and it's already making me feel nuts. You're strong to be semi-sane being there."

"Strong?"

"Yeah. Most people would be doing drugs all the time if they went there. You did them—like an idiot—the first time today. You're strong and maybe even smart. You make dumb decisions, Caldo. Thank God you've got me in your life now."

She drove into my neighborhood, impressed, "You live in a pretty nice neighborhood. You'd think your parents could have sent you to an actual good private school."

"An Italian dentist and a Jewish mother are the cheapest people you'll ever meet in your life. They got a discount on it. I was the guinea pig for the school—student zero."

The car stopped in my driveway. "That sucks, Caldo. You deserve to be a little bit emo even if you're a privileged white guy. What are you going to tell your mom?"

"I'll figure that out tomorrow. I need to get some sleep and get ready for my new first job."

"Yeah, you can't fuck this one up."

"I won't. You're a good mentor, I guess."

"Show up tomorrow. Deal?"

"Deal."

"Good luck!" she called out, driving off as I took the keys out of my pants pockets. I took a deep breath and opened the door. Right on the click I heard, "How was work? Tell me all about it."

I needed to sleep. I was crashing so hard but mustered out, "It was so good. I'll tell you all about it. I need to change first. Working is hard. I feel tired."

"That's how a man feels after a good day of work, Joseph," Mom said. "I'm proud of you."

Oof. Those words almost hurt as much as Alexia not saying I love you back, but I was too tired to come clean.

I headed straight upstairs, took off my shoes and collapsed on the bed. I could feel my body ready to collapse. I'd escape from the reality that was my life for a little bit. No wonder David Lynch was obsessed with dreams. My thoughts raced less about Mom being pissed and more about what I would make as a film—also was Valerie my only friend now? I needed to dream this away and hope tomorrow was somehow a better day.

Act 3: Scene 6

Waking Into Another Nightmare, An Angry Jewish Mother

That night, I got attacked by my own dreams.

In one, I was in a college classroom trying to code naked, wearing nothing but the fig leaf of Adam. Then, Alexia walked in as the professor but as a raging drunk. She lit a Marlboro Black and kicked over the lectern with a neon green stiletto. I climbed into my computer monitor to hide and then the dream ended. But the implication was that I was trapped in cyberspace forever.

Waking up, the nightmare continued with Mom shaking the lapels of my pajama top and screaming in my face. "Joseph Caldo! Joseph Paul Caldo! Get up now! Look what's on YouTube!"

I considered pretending I was dead but sat up and looked at the blur of her iPhone. There was my high ass rolling around in the dirty grocery store like it was some rancid sex club. "Shit. I can explain."

"Please do! Your ex-boss emailed this to me this morning. Congrats, Joseph. You already have over a thousand views!"

"I got drugged. I got drugged!"

She stopped the video and said sternly, "Don't bullshit me, Joseph. You did drugs! And probably cause of a girl. You make your worst decisions cause of girls!"

Jewish moms were like fortune tellers sometimes. I sat up and stared out my window, a shitty mix of regret and raw sewage bubbling up in my stomach. "Yeah, Mom. It was a girl. She gave me something. She said it would help me with the job."

"I'm sure she did!"

"Aw man, I messed up, Mom. I really messed up with this."

Mom put her phone away. "You really did, Joseph! You'll never get a job now with this on the Internet. And if colleges find this, you're done. I'm so disappointed in you. I honestly think we should skip college and have you enroll in a coding school online cause you can't even handle a K-Mart cashier job!"

What she was saying hurt and I wanted to stand up for myself. Wasn't part of coming-of-age making mistakes? Where was her forgiveness? I deserved to say that I missed making videos with my camera, that I didn't want to be a tech bro, that I was an artist, and that I was deprived of connection in this world I felt so isolated in. I didn't ask to be born. That part was her fault. Then sending me to that stupid school only made things worse. But instead I said, "I have a job interview today. A real job. I have an interview in like an hour and a half."

"Don't lie to me, Joseph. Enough!"

"I'm serious."

"How is this even possible? Who the hell lured you in after what happened yesterday? Were you summoned to the streets?"

"The new girl from school set it up. The one Connie assigned to be my mentor or whatever. She picked me up from K-Mart and said her cousin had a job that needed to be filled right away. I took her up on it. I was trying to right the wrong I did before you knew about it. I'm sorry. I screwed up really bad."

"This is new. I've never seen you try to right a wrong."

"It's true, Mom. It's true."

She backed off and smoothed her shirt. "This is. Well, progress. I think."

"Thanks?" I wasn't sure if it was a compliment.

"What is the job?"

I wiped my eyes. "It's working with children."

She looked proud. "Really?"

"It's being the Chuck E. Cheese mouse."

She tried to hold a smile but it shifted to a smirk.

"And I'm even going to study afterwards with the mentor girl for our Shakespeare project that Connie is having us do. I'm trying to make things right."

"Do you and this girl like each other?"

"Trust me. She doesn't like me and most of the time I can't stand her, but she's pretty good at this whole mentoring thing. And maybe this will even turn into a friendship."

Mom sighed, relieved. "I'm glad that school is finally doing something positive for you."

I strangely agreed. Everything that had been swirling around in my head: school, women, my life. My mom rarely showed empathy or any signals she was a human and not some angry robot, so when she did it felt really good. I wanted to share more with her, but then I remembered she'd seen a video of me doing weird shit with dolls. Oh god. I prayed it wouldn't go viral.

Mom clocked my anxiety and shifted her tone gentler. "Why don't we talk more at breakfast with your father? I'm disappointed but pleased to see you trying to fix your mistakes. It's a sign of some kind of maturity. And I'm worried about you. I'm tough on you, but I want you to be happy."

She left and shut the door and I threw on the same lame job interview outfit I'd worn a few days ago. Mom was eating her keto oatmeal while Dad was looking at the 'K-Mart Worker Really Loves Dolls' video. I shamefully played with my scrambled eggs until Dad put the phone down.

"I don't really know what to say, Joseph." His eyes were wide. "I knew you had struggles, but doing drugs for the first time on the first day of your job. What were you thinking, son? Seriously, what the hell were you thinking?"

"I wasn't thinking. I've been so upset and lonely about Alexia and the girl flirted with me and I did Ecstasy with her. It was super dumb. I self-destructed or something. I wasn't even that into her."

"Joseph, it doesn't matter if you weren't into her or not. You don't try a drug on your first day of work! This is common sense. Come on, you gotta grow up. You can't keep messing up good opportunities. You're not a kid anymore."

It was like we were all realizing that adulthood was coming and none of us had confidence that I would be able to handle it.

"And now the only job he can get is being the mouse at Chuck E. Cheese. The mouse! And it's not even set in stone that he'll get it," Mom chimed in.

Dad to the rescue: "Why don't you let Joseph and I talk. Just us."

I appreciated the guy time, but it bummed me out that Dad and I only talked when I either got heartbroken or tried Ecstasy while spooning some K-Mart dolls. We never just, like, went to brunch and a movie.

He sipped his coffee and finally spoke. "I don't even want to know how you already got a job offer to be the Chuck E. Cheese mouse. What I want to know is what's going on with you, Joseph. Tell me what's going on."

I stared at the ceiling fan.

"I'm not a mind reader. Tell me why you're acting out. Are you worried about your future? Do you need more attention?"

"I don't know, Dad. I feel freaked out. Like, all the time." My eyes welled up. Dad put his hand on mine. There wasn't anything more uncomfortable than crying in front of your dad. "You're going to push through. You're already pushing through, by being willing to get another job, and a lousy one at that—it shows you're pushing through."

That opened the floodgates. I wept.

"It's okay to make mistakes. Even really dumb ones, but things are starting to matter. Choices you make now are going to matter more. Are you figuring out what matters to you? Cause well. That's what matters."

I wasn't ready to drop everything on him: that after being with Alexia I knew I didn't want to be isolated from everyone and everything anymore and my buried dream of maybe doing film got stirred up again, that I was trying to save up to get a new camera and maybe even pay for school but I wasn't really sure if I was going to do it cause the idea of making films again freaked me out and I had no real belief in myself. I should have shared all this with my father. This was the time to do it, but I could only say, "I think I'm starting to figure out what matters."

"That's all you can do. So, are you really going to be the mouse? Chuck E.? Is that the mouse's name?"

"Yeah, I'm going to be Chuck E. I really gotta get going. Mom's gonna give me a ride back to my car at K-Mart."

"Did this talk help?"

"It did. Thanks, Dad."

Act 3: Scene 7

The Noble Duties of Rodent Impersonation

After the awkward drive to K-Mart with Mom, I got out of her car and got into my own car to drive to the interview. I thought about my dad. It felt good opening up to him. Maybe my parents were actual people.

My life had totally changed in a week. Next, I'd become a mouse.

I got off the highway and turned into a small shopping center with a Publix and GameStop. Almost all of the South Florida shopping centers looked the same. The parking lot was pretty full but I found a spot near the Chuck E. Cheese entrance. I got out and walked to the smiling mouse on the front door. As I caught my reflection in the door, I couldn't distinguish myself from a mouse. I was perfect for the part.

Walking in the establishment, I found the familiar cocktail of yelling children, grandmothers picking pineapples out of the salad bar, stoned pizza cutters, and dead-eyed dads treating the arcade like a casino. Tattered and forgotten paper tickets were scattered across the geometric carpet. What a waste. Being in

Chuck E. Cheese as a near-adult felt like witnessing the desecration of mankind on our planet firsthand. It felt like yesterday my mom pawned me into a game of Skee-Ball. Back before she hated my grumpy guts.

But maybe I liked the sacrilege of humanity. Wow. Maybe even loved it. It was nice to see kids acting like kids, not like the asshole geniuses at my school. Their cheers didn't suck. They felt like medicine. Like rare, top-shelf, controlled substances. Maybe I needed to be around happy families. I kept people-watching, addicted to their copious joy. But then my intestines ruptured.

Tony mother-loving Rizzio.

Playing *Mortal Kombat* 3. Except like a douche! Out of all the families that could be having a birthday party at Chuck E. Cheese, it had to be Tony Rizzio's Italian mob. It couldn't be easy and simple!

I swear the Capital-U-Universe or whoever was up there was rubbing their hands together, waiting to make my every trial ten times harder than it should have been. Or maybe South Florida was cursed and we were all pre-destined to live in hell. Probably both.

Luckily, Tony was too busy going hard with *Mortal Kombat* to notice me. He won the match as Scorpion and did a fatality on Kano while screaming at the screen, "I'll kill anyone!"

Shit.

I ducked my head and walked past the ball pit. I was pretty sure he didn't see me, and I found the door that said 'manager' in dim gray letters near the bathrooms.

I knocked on it and heard, "Come in!"

I opened the door and saw a nerdy Puerto Rican guy in his late twenties eating a piece of pizza. He looked a little like Valerie, with similar glasses and eyes.

"Hey. I'm here for the interview."

"Oh, hey. Valerie's friend, Joseph Caldo, right?"

"Yes, sir. Good to meet you."

"Chill, dude. You don't gotta call me sir, man. I'm Jorge. Happy to meet you, cause I really need a mouse."

"Happy to be here." I said even though I was never happy.

"Good, man. This job is hard to fill. My little cousin is the best. Right?" So proud of that girl, man. She's gonna be a professor one day. She makes our family so proud."

Oy, vey. Couldn't everyone shut up? She was great. We all knew it. But he kept on anyway. "So when do I get to become Mr. Cheese?"

"It's Chuck E. Cheese, man. It's a simple gig. No different than working for Disney World in a Mickey Mouse costume. You just gotta show up."

"I can do that."

"You gotta show and also speak in a squeaky voice. You can do that, right?"

"I guess."

"Well, don't be shy. Let me hear you."

"Stay out of my territory," I said in a high-pitched Mickey Mouse voice, not sure why I quoted *Breaking Bad*.

"Sound a little nicer, but that's good. Last thing. Can you not swear at children? No matter what? This job has an opening because a guy called a mean little girl the C-word."

"Wow. That's hardcore."

"Corporate was pissed. I can't have that again. You gotta promise me you won't ever curse. Like ever."

"Once again, I can easily do that. I deal with very annoying children at our school, and have never said anything offensive to them." This was only half true considering I shouted at them basically every day.

"Good. Well, we'll find out if you really can, cause I would like to give you a test run today."

"Today? Like now?"

"Yes. Just for this lunch party. Think of it as a tryout for the role of Chuck E. Cheese."

"I have to meet Valerie later today to study, but I'm free now."

"Good. Let's do it." Without another word, he got up and handed me the infamous mouse suit, the costume I'd wear during all the shenanigans to come. "You can change here. These people booked the party a while ago. Let's get straight to business because I don't have to give them half off if Chuck E. comes out. It's easy. You say fun stuff in a mouse voice and keep the kids satiated."

"What's a mouse voice sound like?"

"Like a mouse. Now hurry up." He pointed to an area around a big TV where kids looked hungry and hyper. "If anything goes wrong, I'll come rescue you."

"Do things often go wrong?"

"It's what it is, my man. All types of folks can be cruel but when you're the mouse you can't be cruel back. You'd need human intervention. Respect the customers. That's the only rule for our rodents."

As soon as I got in costume and emerged into what was meant to be a better life, I spotted Tony Rizzio. Yes, only my karma could induce a coincidence that sinister. Damn it. There he sat with a group of kids and a terrifying fifty-something Italian couple. His parents, I assumed.

How was I supposed to act professional? Jorge had literally just said to not be mean or cruel, but how? He didn't mention what to do if I came across my sworn enemy. Seeing Tony's stupid face brought back all of those horrible memories from high school. Even worse, the Alexia feelings returned. This asshole was with her and I was in a fucking mouse costume. It wasn't fair!

Ugh. I imagined him holding Alexia in their smoky, smoldering, troubled bond and I didn't know which was more upsetting:

A) Tony's bullying

B) Tony my nemesis having sex with Alexia

C) Me never having sex with Alexia again

D) All of the above

Can you hear me circling all of the above in the squeaky highlighter of my brain?

Maybe this was a test from the fates to be a better man than Tony instead of equally as petty.

I left the office and walked toward the party. I stopped by Jorge who said, "Do your thing. I gotta do some accounting work in the office. Grab me if you have any issues."

Only a few minutes before, he'd promised to protect my life if there was any trouble. But I didn't want to rock the boat. In a squeaky high voice: "Okie-dokie. Sounds good, boss."

"You got it. Now go be Chuck E. Cheese."

He went back into his office leaving me with the kids. They saw me and started clapping and cheering. I made a little spin move and clapped my hands, and did a weird dance like the *Gangnam Style* guy. I waved at a little kid who looked exactly like Tony, and I said to him in the mouse voice, "Happy Birthday, little guy.

Welcome to Chuck E. Cheese. Let's have a round of applause for the birthday boy!"

The kids screamed and started dancing crazy like bad dubstep was playing.

"It's this little boy's birthday. What a great day. All birthdays are special. Let's have another round of applause. The birthday boy is so cool. Isn't he cool!" Impressed by my dissonance. Little did they know that through mouse eyes I sent hateful flames toward Tony with my most fearful stare. Tony didn't bother to engage yet, busy on his cellular. Ew. He was probably texting Alexia. His hands were probably all greasy on the keyboard. "You're so much cooler than your big brother. He's a real nerd dork," I added.

The kids started chanting. "Nerd dork! Nerd dork! Nerd dork!"

I knew I should stop. This was exactly what Jorge had told me five seconds ago not to do. But the words kept coming out.

"When you're a big boy you will probably not live at home and be super cool, unlike your nerd dork brother, who smells like spoiled cheese."

Tony glared at me like he always used to before bullying me. "Alright, ha-ha. Why don't you shut your mouth up, or."

"Or you'll attack a poor, defenseless mouse? You wouldn't let him hurt me, would you, kids?"

"No!" They screamed like little loyal soldiers. "No way!"

"WE LOVE YOU, CHUCK E!" some rabid kid screamed.

"For your birthday gift you can say something that will embarrass your brother. I let you do this in the name of Cheese Mountain," I ordered and twirled around like I'd cast a spell.

The sadistic children leered and jeered. For once, kids' horrible desire to bully could be put to good use as Tony's face turned bright red.

His little brother chimed in: "His girlfriend dumped him. Mom says it's because he lives at home and he cried like a dork!"

Tony stood up. "Shut the fuck up, Nicholas, and shut your fucking mouth you stupid mouse, if you know what's good for you."

"Boo! Boo!"

Tony looked like he was about to cry. Hell yes, she'd dumped his ass!

Damn, this was like real revenge. Like exposing Watergate. Or something. In my best Deep Throat not-mouse voice: "Thank God Alexia left you."

"Wait. Caldo?"

Not deep enough. I shouldn't have said her name. "Nope, my name is Chuck E."

Tony got up and pushed me. I stumbled back. "She said she wasn't even that into you! At least she liked me. She pitied you. She'll come back. Messed up girls like her always do, but she'll never be with you again."

I relived that horrible pain of Alexia not feeling the same. It almost hurt more because what he said was probably true. I could only go lower and try to make him feel worse.

"Peaking in high school and Alexia dumping me would make me act like a meanie too!"

"I didn't peak in high school. I'm putting my mixtape up on SoundCloud! And it's fire, you little bitch!" He stood up and raised his fist at me. I ducked down, feeling a panic attack coming on.

"Help, children! Help me!" I said, somehow still in character. "He's threatening and cursing and desecrating the mouse kingdom!"

Jorge walked out of his office. "Hey!" he shouted and pointed to the sign that read, *No threatening to hit the mouse*. "You have to leave, sir. We can't have that in front of the children."

"This is bullshit! That asshole started it!"

"Leave right now or I'm calling the cops!"

"Fuck all of you. You're dead! You're fucking dead, bitch boy!"

My private thoughts screamed for help, but I threw up jazz hands and said, "Well, kids! Who wants pizza?"

Act 3: Scene 8

Ye E. Cheese Kingdom Under Siege

After the party ended I handed the mouse costume to Valerie's cousin. It had felt kind of good and kind of bad to bully a bully, but damn it hit me now that it was dumb to almost lose my job to mess with him. It was weird too, cause it had felt really good at first, but now I felt a kind of crash from that high.

I felt a little bad about it, but should I really feel bad about it? Was I as bad as Tony?

The worst part was all the Alexia stuff was back in full force. It wasn't worth it to hear what he'd told me. I could picture her telling him those exact words, and they hurt more than any punch Tony had ever thrown at me.

God, was I ever going to get over Alexia Marcos? Was I always going to shit on every opportunity that came my way?

These thoughts went in and out of my head as Jorge typed in my hours. "You did really good for your first time. The kids were happy, and you survived a mouse threatening and a curse out."

"Does that really happen a lot?"

"Man, before I officially hire you, I should tell you that stuff like that does happen a lot. But you handled it right, and you didn't fight back. You can't, and unfortunately you will have to deal with assholes. It's always the angry twenty-something white guys that want to start shit. Almost every time."

"He said he was a SoundCloud rapper. Those guys really struggle in life and are very angry."

"I imagine so, man. I imagine so."

"It did feel good to make the kids happy. I kind of like being Chuck E."

"Good, cause you got the job. I'm going to put you on the payroll Monday for afternoons, night shifts, and weekends."

"Oh. Great! Thank you!"

"All good, my man. I can tell you're one tough motherfucker, you need to be to do this gig. I can tell you've been through some stuff. You'll be fine. And tell Valentina hello from her favorite cousin. Give it here."

"I will," I said and gave him a fist pound.

I felt good for a second as I walked out of the Chuck E. Cheese, but fear gripped me, picturing Tony Rizzio waiting outside to beat me up, high school style. I crept out toward my car but he was nowhere to be found.

I got in and felt relief that I'd survived being the mouse. It hit me that I'd been through a lot in the last week. I felt like I'd lived more in the last week than I'd lived in my entire life. I still felt like a mess, but I also felt like I could push through things, like Dad had been talking about. I hoped this made it easier to do this Shakespeare bullshit with Valerie.

I put her address into my phone and started driving.

It was only a few miles away but it was the bad side

of Delray, as Mom called it. I put on the death metal station. I didn't like death metal, but I'd learned no one messed with weird white guys who listened to it.

I kept on driving until I made a turn and Siri's unmistakable robotic voice told me I was one mile from Valerie's. I drove through the neighborhood, which was definitely different from where I lived, and saw one guy on the corner wearing yellow and black with dealer vibes. I drove past him and Siri told me I would approach it on my right in half a mile. I pulled into the driveway of a small blue house that could use a paint job and a new roof. I got out of the car and walked to the front door. I wasn't looking forward to doing this whole studying thing, but I owed Valerie big time.

Act 3: Scene 9

Of Mothers Most Wise and Oversharing Most Awkward

I knocked on the door and a Latina woman with bouncy black curls answered. "You must be Caldo. Come on in."

"Hello, madam. Good to meet you."

She put out her hand and smiled, "Oh please don't make me feel old with the madam stuff. I'm Rios. Valerie says she's mentoring you and working on a project with you for Miss Connie."

"Yeah. I'm not like a problem kid or anything. She's more like a tutor to help me achieve my genius and whatnot. Not that I think of myself as a Kanye West student of life or anything like that."

"That's good. You're funny. Valerie didn't tell me that, but she did say that everyone at your school except you is a psychopath or belongs in a mental hospital. Is this true? She has a tendency to exaggerate."

"Eh, it's kind of true to be honest."

"Wow. I really thought Valerie was being dramatic."

"Nah. We're sharing our school with deviants and the mentally ill."

"Even if there are deviants and nut cases, public school isn't much better. Trust me, I survived Miami Senior High in the nineties—we had actual gang fights during lunch. The teachers at your school are so impressive. I love Miss Connie, and Mr. Wilkins the biology teacher. Both brilliant PhDs. They're the kind of teachers that Valerie deserves and needs. She's so intelligent, and I think one-on-one tutoring can get her truly prepared to enter a master's program in her third year in college."

"Yeah, I don't always agree with her methods but Miss Connie is a great teacher. That's why Mom had me go there. To unlock my potential."

"Miss Connie is a saint. She helped get the scholarship-mentor program started and knew of Valentina from judging a debate contest she won."

"Well, your daughter is super smart so she'll get a ton of them."

"Thank you. Please keep an eye on her so she doesn't burn herself out. Kid's got more Type A personality than a room full of cardiac surgeons."

"Sure. Valerie is a cool girl, I got her back."

"I appreciate it, Caldo. That's the first I've heard of someone calling Valerie 'cool.' Usually it's 'terrifying' or 'intense.' It's nice to hear."

Valerie came in wearing a blue baggy t-shirt and comfy looking blue pants and said, "Being called cool by the new Chuck E. Cheese doesn't really mean much, Mom. I got Caldo a job with Cousin Jorge."

Rios snickered. "You really are going to be the new mouse? Ay, Dios mío. I worked at a McDonald's Play-

Place when I was seventeen. The things kids do to those ball pits. . . you'll see."

"Chuck E. Cheese is about to become an expert on Shakespeare," Valerie said as she slouched against the wall, unenthused. "Come on, Caldo, let's get this over with." She led me to her room like a warden escorting a prisoner.

We got to her room and I sat down at her desk. Over her bed were posters of Frida Kahlo and bell hooks and Christopher Marlowe, which made sense, but I was surprised that she had an *Amélie* poster. The one where Amélie's a kid and has a raspberry on each finger.

Hm. I didn't take Valerie as someone who'd like a French art film. Her room was spotless save for a stack of Cornell brochures and SATs and an aneurysm-inducing bulletin board featuring daily to-do lists (torn to the date we were on—who does that?) and a whiteboard plastered with magnets of book covers, of course, including one of *The Bell Jar*. There was a handwritten note in purple bubble handwriting from a friend that read:

Be ThE vAlEdIcToRiAn && tHe ToUgH3$t BiiZn@tcH <3

"Your room looks like a chaos magic spell to get into a college." I took it all in. "But I gotta say, the *Amélie* poster is throwing me off. Feels off-brand."

"Are you about to be a mansplaining film nerd about *Amélie*? Of all films?"

"No." The truth was I didn't like seeing it there because it reflected back the part of myself I needed to repress. To resist it, I gave my speech. "I usually love art films. I really do. But I couldn't stand that girl. She was so annoying. It was a pretentious film too, and I love most pretentious art films, but it was lame. It was like eating nothing but French pastries for two hours. It would have been better as a short."

"In other words, you loved it and watched it enough times to say that."

I fumed.

"Let me guess. You don't like *Chocolat* either."

"No. These are mainstream films disguised as quirky indie stuff to make normies think they like alt-stuff. It's fake indie and *Amélie* is the worst of it. She's the manic pixie dream girl getting the starring role."

"*Amélie* is one of the only films that I've seen that captured the same magic of a great book. Films are always second to literature but *Amélie* felt like reading a book on the screen."

I didn't know *Amélie* had been a book. I'd have to check it out at the library. "That's total bullshit. The book is way better."

She died laughing. "The irony is you're a male Amélie."

"What?! I am not a male Amélie. That is the most emasculating thing anyone has ever said to me."

"I'd be friends with her!"

"Friends don't tell their guy friends they're like Amélie. There's no such thing as a manic pixie dream boy."

"Okay, Mr. Reddit Cinema. What is your brilliant idea for our Shakespeare remix and how it connects to our current lives? You can talk shit but can you create something new?"

"I don't know. Damn, you are right." I sputtered. "I am good at talking shit about films but not at thinking of new ideas. Oh no, I've become one of those film guys. Shit."

"Stop before it's too late, Caldo. It's not too late."

I tried to think of something interesting, but all I could think of was making a post on r/AskReddit to ask Reddit why I couldn't think of anything interesting.

"I get it. I'm good at explaining the points or goals of art and literature but I'm not good at creating them. But come on! Care to share some of your manic pixie dream boy inspo?"

She was such a goof—student council energy but with a dash of refreshing weirdness.

She was on a role. "I know!" she said. "We can make mood boards for inspiration. Let's go to the dollar store."

"No! It doesn't have to come to that. Marvel movies are going to be popular forever. What if we did like a Marvel version of *Macbeth*, everyone is obsessed, isn't *Iron Man* like *King Lear* or some bullshit?"

"That is a terrible idea and not even in the romance genre. Give me something to work with here. Before you got blocked or whatever, what did you do?"

"I didn't think. I just did stuff with a camera."

"Alright, you've seen a million films or whatever. What do people do in them to get creatively inspired?"

I scratched my head to think and replied, "In the movies I've seen artists and scientists or whatever pace around and then get a brilliant idea."

"Well do that then, cause I don't have anything and we're not going to bomb this project."

I started pacing around the room, but that felt weird so I stopped and looked at Valerie's desk. The only interesting thing was a picture frame face down. "What are you doing? Caldo, this is weird. Stop. Leave that down."

But I couldn't resist. She didn't get to me fast enough. I picked up the picture frame. I saw a very built, fridge-body dude who looked like an evil Tim Tebow with his arm around Valerie and a face that screamed: I'm awesome and you know it.

"Ooh shit. This is the ex-boyfriend," I said with a little shock.

She panicked. "Yes, but it doesn't matter. It's over. Or mostly over."

She came over as I stared into his money-green eyes. He was a total Blockbuster and I hated him. "He looks exactly how you described him at IHOP."

"Ugh, my taste in men comes straight from the 'toxic relationships' tag on Tumblr."

Her and everybody else. I set the photo back on her nightstand.

I could tell Valerie wanted to flip it down again but left it up and stared at it.

"We could cut his face out of the picture," I offered. "That always helps. It's a good picture of you with a nice nature scene behind it, otherwise. I like that ocean view. Look. There's even a baby seagull. Let's cut him out. It'll be you and a baby seagull."

For the first time since I'd known her, she looked vulnerable. Not annoyed or superior or impatient—sad. "He was definitely a jerk, but we had something, and there was, you know, passion. And I liked how I felt with him. He's the only guy I've been with and we did it a lot, though, he always called it banging, which really annoyed me."

"Aw shit, Valerie was getting her swerve on with a douchey Tim Tebow."

"Shut up, Caldo."

"Can I ask something really inappropriate?"

"What do you want to know about me and Brad?"

"Oh god. His name was Brad."

She stared back blankly. I kept talking.

"So, like, Brad looks like he's pretty big down there. Does it really matter? Does, you know, does being big down there really matter to girls? Cause on the internet I hear differing views. I want to know the truth. This mentoring right here, I'm not trying to be weird, I swear. You're always honest."

"We're supposed to be talking about Shakespeare, not about my ex's pinga. I don't know. It depends on the girl. I mean he was 6'3 and had an above-average one. It wasn't the most important thing but it didn't hurt, either. Figuratively." She covered her eyes. "God, I've watched too many Chad Michael Murray movies. The culture basically brainwashed us to fall for emotionally unavailable F Boys."

"This is a pervasive cultural issue," I said.

She missed the irony. "Exactly! I literally wrote a debate case about toxic masculinity in teen movies last year and won nationals, but here I am sounding like every girl on Instagram who falls for an asshole who brags about the size of his dick but doesn't even know how to use the metric system. . ."

Valerie's mother entered the doorway, holding a tray of Cuban sandwiches. "Are we talking about a certain Shakespeare character?"

Valerie groaned. "Yeah, Mom."

I tried to help smooth out the tense moment. "Julius Caesar. He was very well-endowed but bad at math. That's why Cleopatra was so into him."

Her mom put the sandwiches near the picture and

joined us. "I like him, Valerie. You two need to hang out more. He's funny and nice, not like that Neanderthal ex of yours. Brad was so rude and entitled every time he came over. Reminded me of every finance jerk I dated in my twenties before I got smart."

"Valerie, you should listen to your mother. She's very wise," I added. "And never date white guys named Brad. That's a good policy. No disrespect to Bradley Cooper. He's an underrated director and actor."

Ms. Diaz laughed again. I wished I could be this likable to girls instead of their moms. "Trust me, mijo, I learned that lesson the hard way. Dated three Brads, two Chads, and a Connor. All disasters. Maybe you should be Valerie's mentor, Joseph."

"Brad wasn't that bad."

Ms. Diaz raised an eyebrow, "Honey, I worked two jobs to put myself through nursing school while dating guys who thought Axe body spray was a personality trait. Brad's not special because he can throw a football."

"I still stand firm that you should go to your old school's dance," she continued. "Maybe you can talk some sense into Valerie, Joseph. She was supposed to go to a dance this coming week with her friends from the debate team."

"I imagine them to be single as well," I said.

"Yes, they are, but they're great girls. Since Brad is taking someone else, Valerie isn't going and I think she should go."

"It's fine, Mom. No necesito ir."

"Look, mija, you always talk about feminism and empowerment and being all woke but you're not living it if you don't go, mijita. A strong woman can go to a dance alone, whether their ex will be there or not."

I started clapping. "That was moving, Ms. Diaz. I see where she gets her debate skills."

Valerie rolled her eyes. "It's fine. I really don't want to go."

"Your choice. But I'm speaking from experience here—don't let some boy dictate your social life. I did that once and missed my senior prom. Still regret it. And from the sound of things, I don't think there are going to be any dances at the new school."

"I don't know. You, Fane, and Charles could have a dance," I joked.

"Shut up, Caldo. I'm fine."

"If you asked Shakespeare, he'd tell you to go," her mom said. "Right, Joseph?"

"I honestly don't know what he would say, but I think she should totally go. You should go be with your home girls. Not going would be like a tragedy, but a pretty lame one. So yeah, I think you're right, Ms. Diaz. I think Shakespeare would totally tell Valerie to go to that dance, he only liked epic tragedies, not lame ones."

A look of death from Valerie. "No. He'd tell me to go poison myself rather than go to the dance with my ex and his new girlfriend."

Act 3: Scene 10

Send Forth Thine Finest Limo

Ms. Diaz left us alone, and Valerie stared at the Brad photo for a little too long.

We finally got to working on our Shakespeare in the Present Day project and Valerie's eyes glazed over as I kept rattling off ideas. I finally said a terrible one to make sure she was paying attention, "*Romeo and Juliet*, but with snails. We can, like, make the snails talk." She ignored what was a genius idea and stayed fixed at the wall.

"You've been all emo since your mom came in. We both can't be weird and emo. Then we'd be screwed for the project and in life."

She looked like she was going to tell me that she had an incurable disease. "I lied to my mom."

"That's a Shakespeare retelling idea? He had a play about lying to moms?"

"No, you dummy. About the prom."

"Oh. Why?"

"It's complicated." She got frazzled. No more of the 'I'm better than everyone' vibe she always beamed out.

She wanted to run away behind her square glasses. "I can't go alone, Caldo. I can't, but I do want to go to the prom."

I shrugged, not getting the big deal. "So go to prom with your friends, then."

She sighed even louder. "Oh, fourth wave feminists. Forgive me, but I can't go without a date. Brad is going to have a date, and his date is the girl that he cheated on me with. And I can't. He's always made fun of me, cause my friends weren't cool. If I go with them, he's going to make out with that stupid pretty blanca bitch and I'll be miserable."

"Wait a sec. You still really like him?"

"Maybe."

"So that is a major yes."

"I don't want to like him. OH MY GOD. I hate that he's with that mean Cara Delevingne wannabe. She's such a bimbo, and I know she seduced him. I know he didn't really want to cheat. He really does love me and I love him, and I couldn't let it go that he cheated. He said he was sorry and it was a mistake, but no matter how much I wanted to. I couldn't let it go, but a part of me. A part that I hate, still wants to be with him, and I want to go to the dance."

"Yo, I relate. Big time, though I think I'm sort of getting over Alexia or at least accepting it's not gonna happen."

Was I getting over her? After the Tony thing today, hearing what she supposedly said about me, it hurt but it didn't destroy me like it would have a week ago.

"I need a date. I can't go alone."

"Valerie, I don't have any friends I can hook you up with."

"No, Caldo, you freaking dummy. I'm talking about you. Jesus. Hello!?"

"Oh. Me. Me? Are you serious? Like you want me as your date?"

"I'm not into you, Caldo. I need a date. I'd like to sort of make Brad jealous. And maybe make him admit he wants me back and maybe even take me back."

"And you are picking me to do this?" I asked, realizing I was self-negging brutally, bro.

My mind flashed to everything Alexia had gone through with Tony, everything I'd gone through chasing her. Did I really want to help Valerie do the same thing?

"Yeah, you. Yes, Brad is classically way better looking than you, but like I said: you're a pixie dream boy aura will totally mess with his head. Trust me."

"I appreciate that. Thanks."

"You got the cute goofy white guy thing, which is totally in now. If you were a chick, you'd totally have asymmetrical bangs."

I nodded. "Asymmetrical bangs do elevate that hotness status."

"I'm asking as your friend. Would you take me to my school prom?" I let out a deep sigh, not really loving this idea and getting a bunch of anxiety about pissing off that evil Tim Tebow doppelgänger. Valerie had saved my ass last night, got me this job, and had been the only real friend I'd had in forever.

"Come on, Caldo. If you had a real shot with Alexia, wouldn't you take action?"

"Yeah, probably. If she was into me, I'd do anything."

"Well, that is what I'm doing. For better or worse, Brad is my Alexia. I still miss him and I still want to be with him. I know because he still thumbs-up and thumbs-down my Facebook posts."

"Damn. This is some real Shakespeare shit."

"We'll get back to that, in a sec. So can you go?"

"Will there be a limo?"

"Yes."

I liked the idea of going to prom in a limo. "Then yes. I always wanted to ride in one of those fancy things and go to a. . . fancy thing. You can pick me up at the retirement home."

"You'll be with your grandmother? That is freaking cute as hell. I love her, she's so funny. My debate team señoritas will think that is so sweet."

"I guess I'm going to prom."

"Thank you, Caldo. This means a lot."

I nodded and blushed but I wasn't sure why. Maybe it was because this felt like the first time someone had really needed me for something important.

Watching Valerie all keyed up like that, I got a burst of inspiration. I had a real idea for this stupid Shakespeare project and shared, "We should use our lives as the assignment for Connie. We can go balls to the wall meta. Share whatever happens at the dance and combine it with *Romeo and Juliet*."

Valerie sat up straighter, her academic brain kicking in. "Wait. You're onto something. Think about it—*Romeo and Juliet* is about young people making terrible decisions because of love, right? And we're both doing exactly that."

"I don't think my decisions are terrible. Well, many of them are. But yes. Meta. Postmodern. Connie loves all that nonsense."

"She's going to eat this up. Plus, it'll help us figure out our actual strategy for Wednesday. Like, what's our endgame here? How do we make Brad jealous without you getting your ass kicked?"

"Great, so I'm definitely going to get my ass kicked."

"Not if we're smart about it." She started scribbling notes. "See, this is why Shakespeare is still relevant. Same problems, different costumes."

Somewhere between the IHOP pancakes and that moment, Valerie had stopped being my annoying mentor and became my actual friend. Someone who rescued me from K-Mart, got me a job, and was now letting me help her with her own mess.

"You know what's weird? A week ago I thought my life was ending because of Alexia. Now I'm sitting here helping you chase your ex, and it doesn't feel like the end of the world anymore."

"That's character development, Caldo. Shakespeare would be proud."

"Or he'd kill us all off in Act V."

"Let's hope we're in a comedy, not a tragedy."

Nothing had gone the way I'd expected. But maybe that wasn't always a bad thing.

"Let's pass Junior English Lit and give the performance of a lifetime by getting your quarterback. . . back."

Act 4

Act 4: Scene 1

Of Meta-Modern Going On and On (Unlike the Titanic)

On Monday, I drove to school thinking about the insane past weekend and the crazy week ahead. I couldn't believe I was going to prom or that Valerie and I had conjured such a genius idea for our project.

Something I'd learned in my many, many hours watching indie films was that if things weren't flowing, just go meta and make it seem like that was the point all along. I wished I could videotape what we'd do for the project for a possible film submission, but it was going to be a shit show and meta-stuff usually sucked. I wouldn't be able to afford a decent camera till at least a month's work as the mouse.

I had to think of something good to make for submissions if I was going to do the film school thing. Telling Alexia not to settle had struck a chord with me about film as well, but I was still totally blocked and couldn't picture myself getting behind a camera again. The meta thing was the only real idea I'd had. Maybe I should share this stuff with Dr. Heller?

I felt like I'd sort of switched places with Valerie.

She was way less focused on the project and had been texting me stuff about Brad and the dance. I was starting to realize how nuts people who got stuck on their first love were. She even texted me a pic of the two of them, asking me if she was pretty enough for him. It was weird. Valerie was this badass overachiever feminist chick, but with Brad she'd seen his abs or whatever and acted like a female version of me. Which wasn't a male Amélie! I was unique, dammit!

I pulled off the highway and got on the road to my school. I felt okay, considering. Not good or great, but I felt semi-normal for the first time since post-Alexia sex. I didn't feel great that a video of me doing weird stuff with dolls was out there, but Mom said she'd reported it for copyright infringement cause I was singing that stupid "Baby" song.

Walking in, I ignored the kids yelling insults at me. Life and even little kids could be cruel, but I walked past the slights and entered the school. I passed the other rooms and went to my office door. Miss Connie was already there.

"Mr. Caldo, you look less morose than usual. Productive weekend?"

I sat down and got comfortable. "Surprisingly, yeah. I even met with Valerie for mentoring. She's helped me out. We worked on the Shakespeare project to perform in front of the kids."

"Really?"

"It's gonna be good. Meta and postmodern."

"Postmodernism? Intriguing."

"The kids are smart enough. They'll get our postmodern meta play," I bullshitted, trying to sound smart.

"Hearing you use an actual literary term unironically pleases me. Valerie's already being a positive influence. It's good for you to be around someone of the same intellectual caliber."

"Valerie and me on the same level? Isn't she like a genius? To be fair, she can analyze the hell out of a sonnet but can't wrap her brain around dating a dude that doesn't treat her like Claudius treats Gertrude, all stepdad energy and no respect."

"A surprisingly good Shakespeare metaphor, she is doing her job, though that's a pervasive cultural issue."

"That's what I said! We're onto something, Connie."

Miss Connie briefly face-palmed before reorienting. "Valerie and I. . . she's very smart, has a high IQ and literary knowledge, but she's also extremely hardworking. That's why Mrs. Judy gave out the scholarship. If you worked hard like her, you could do something admirable as well in your life and your studies. I believe that. . . but do you believe that, Mr. Caldo?"

I was thinking about how to answer her when Valerie walked into the room, carrying a stack of books that might topple over at any moment.

"Behold, Caldo, the texts have arrived," she announced dramatically, dropping the pile onto my desk with a thunderous thud. "I grabbed every Shakespeare-related book from the library. Plus SparkNotes, because let's be honest, you're going to need them."

"Ah, Miss Diaz. Just in time. We were discussing your Shakespeare project."

"It's going to be revolutionary." Valerie pushed her glasses up her nose with her index finger. "A postmodern deconstruction of *Romeo and Juliet* set against the backdrop of contemporary teenage hierarchical social structures."

I stared at her blankly. "It's what now?"

"It's about how dating in high school sucks," she translated, rolling her eyes.

"I see you two have found common ground. I'll leave you to it." She headed for the door, pausing to add, "I expect greatness, you two. I shall let Miss Diaz take over the class."

As soon as she was gone, I turned to Valerie. "What the hell was that? 'Contemporary teenage hierarchical social structures'? Are we even doing the same project?"

"Relax, Caldo. That's how you talk to teachers to make them leave you alone. I am a genius, remember?" She smirked. "Even if I do have questionable taste in men."

"Speaking of which, are we still on for Operation Prom Disaster? We're really doing this."

"Don't call it that! It's Operation Make Brad Jealous and Realize What He's Missing."

"That title needs work," I said. "Too many syllables. Not catchy enough for the movie poster. What about Make Brad Jelly?"

"Ha!"

"I'm for realsies. I gotta think of a good hook to show visually. Let my creative juices finally start to flow."

"Let it happen naturally. I have a funny feeling this prom is gonna finally inspire you to get back behind the camera and really have something to say."

"I hope so."

She loved watching me squirm. "Step one: you and I need to practice dancing."

I put up a "this is my no-no square" gesture in protest. "I have to dance? I thought we'd hang out and take pictures and drink spiked punch or whatever."

"No, Caldo. And nobody really spikes the punch.

This isn't the 80s. We're gonna strike some moves and look good doing it, so we make Brad jealous."

"That's still the 80s. Haven't you seen *Dirty Dancing*?"

"Nobody puts Baby in a corner. And you're Baby, Caldo."

"Um. . ." I said, feeling embarrassed about what I was gonna tell her. "I've never danced with a girl. I was too chicken to ask anyone at my cousin's Bar Mitzvah."

"Never?"

"Never ever." I felt lame.

"You really don't know how to dance? Like not even slow dancing? When literally all you do is hang your arms over me and sway back and forth?"

"I have restless leg syndrome, Valerie. It's a serious medical condition that affects millions. Maybe we'd be better off fast dancing like in the videos. That's dry humping, right?"

"No, Caldo. It's not dry humping. ¡Eres tan ignorante!" Valerie was ready to chew my head off, putting me in metaphorical time out. "I'll be right back."

Before I was able to ask what she was doing and where she was going, she brought back Jamie who was entering my room without knocking.

Jamie stood awkwardly in the doorway while Valerie came closer to me. "Are you two like, friends now?"

Valerie answered for both of us. "We can all be friends. I'd like to be friends with you, Jamie."

Jamie went suspicious. "Why?"

"Why not? Chicas gotta stick together."

"Um, okay."

Valerie gave her a wink, and I didn't think Jamie

understood winks were a good thing, but Jamie actually smiled.

I felt like how people treated Jamie showed whether they were good or bad. I was somewhere in the middle, but I could see now that Valerie actually was a good person.

"I need some help from you, Jamie," Valerie continued. "I heard you sing in the bathroom. You're really good."

Jamie shrugged. "I like to sing in the bathroom. . . it helps me go."

"Hey, girl, whatever works. You have an amazing voice, and I'd love it if you sang something for me and Caldo."

"Why?" Jamie asked.

"I have to teach Caldo how to dance and it would be nice if you sang that same song you sang in the bathroom. You know the one, the Céline Dion *Titanic* song."

I didn't think I'd ever seen her smile once. She straightened her spine. "Why, yes. I love to sing."

"You're so good, Jamie, and I promise we won't judge you. We'll be too busy dancing, right, Caldo?"

"Wait. . . we're gonna dance right now?" I asked.

Valerie stood up and put out her hand. "Come on, Caldo. Show me your moves. Let's see how you dance even when things feel super awkward. Cause prom's gonna be super awkward."

"Are you serious? This is ridiculous, Valerie."

"You come on, Caldo," Valerie shot back and held out her hand like she was some Disney princess. "Dance with me, Caldo, and Jamie, sing your heart out."

Jamie cleared her throat and a beautiful voice that

reminded me a little of Ariana Grande came with the first notes.

"Damn, you're pretty good, Jamie. You lead or whatever till I learn."

Valerie placed my hands on her hips and began to move with Jamie's voice. I followed her feet and eyes. She was good at leading, but I could tell she wanted me to take over—this was the only time I'd felt that from her.

I looked down at her. "I'm not terrible at this."

"No, you're not, Caldo. You're decent. She smiled at me while Jamie belted out the famous Her voice filled the room in a way that would make Céline Dion proud. I gave her a twirl.

"If I was with anyone else this would be super romantic," I told her. "You're a romantic, that's why you like middlebrow indie films."

"What of it?"

"It helps me understand you a little more. We're more alike than I thought."

"Brad turns me into this. I get all Caldo-esque."

"I don't think it's Brad. You're a romantic. It's your one and only flaw."

"I'm pretty awesome."

"And with commendable humility."

I took in Jamie's singing, moved. "It's hard to be romantic. We really get hurt, and we get let down. But we're different too. . . with life, you attack it while I hide from it. But with love, I fight for it. . ."

"Maybe, Caldo. But when prom comes around, I guess I'm just like you."

Act 4: Scene 2

Wherein Fame Doth Mock Our Hero Most Cruelly

Valerie and Jamie left. It felt nice to dance but then I kept going back to Miss Connie's question: Why couldn't I be someone like Valerie? Why I struggled to believe in myself. She worked hard and went after anything she wanted—even if it was a douchebro like Brad. Hell, she got Jamie to sing and got me to dance. She had a special way about her and knew how to get things done.

Was this how I was born, or was it people and events that had made me this way? This question felt harder to answer when Fane and Charles came into the room. Fane was holding a phone, smiling, and Charles was showing off his usual creepy smug smile.

Charles stood and started singing a Justin Bieber song, and Fane lifted up her phone and played the scene.

Now it had over 2,654 views on YouTube.

FML.

"They're gonna take it down, copyright infringement."

"This is the best part, when you bring SpongeBob into the mix. I made sure to send it to my boys on 4Chan."

Fane watched me petting Bieber's hair and rubbing SpongeBob's belly. "I don't know what's better, you having a ménage à trois with the dolls or the reactions of the kids. . . How did you do something this stupid, Caldo?"

"Ecstasy and a girl with rainbow hair."

"Tell me Rainbow Brite ended up riding your white horse, bro!" Charles stuck out his knuckles to give me a fist pound.

"No. I don't consent to that."

"So I'm guessing you and the college girl are as dead as Charles' chances of hooking up with Valerie."

I shrugged, trying to block out the pain of the rejection. "Yeah, Alexia and I aren't gonna happen. I've thrown in the white flag and probably won't experience love like that again, maybe ever. . . damn, that really bums me out now that you mentioned it."

Fane groaned. "You're truly a screw-up, Caldo. Even Charles looks down on you."

"Whatever. You know what, Charles? I'm going to a dance with Valerie. I'm gonna go to her prom. She's going with me, the doll guy, not you."

Fane got skeptical and Charles gritted his teeth. "How did this happen? I've been so nice to her and she's been a stuck-up bitch. Or maybe she won't date white guys. This could be reverse racism."

"Just because she won't date you doesn't mean she's a stuck-up bitch, and I'm white too," I asserted.

Charles stared me down like I was the crazy one. "No, you're Jewish, and if a girl isn't a lesbian and doesn't at least give me one date then she's a stuck-up bitch or racist. I've seen memes about this."

"Connie's having her mentor you, Caldo. It's part of her grade to be nice to you."

I shrugged. "Yeah, that's true, Fane, but we already worked on our dancing today, so I'm prepared for prom. . . as her date."

"No way! This is total bullshit!" Charles exclaimed.

"You're her date?" Fane stared me down like a detective struggling to solve a tough case.

"Sort of, she's taking me as a friend for undisclosed reasons, but Charles, I'm riding in a limo with her desperate debate club friends. I probably have at least a 77.9% chance of sleeping with at least two of them."

"I'm gonna ask Connie to be part of Valerie's mentor program. I want to bang desperate debate club chicks too!" Charles said and exited the room.

Fane stayed. "So you and Valerie are going to the dance; it's weird. I don't get it; unless she has an ex-boyfriend and you're there to make him jealous."

"That's pretty much it. You're kind of evil but you have a good brain to see how things work, I'll give you that."

"You're gonna fall for her like a fool. You're a dimwit."

"No, I'm not, I'm not even into her."

She got up to leave. "You're into girls that are too good for you. That's your type."

Act 4: Scene 3

Alas! Shakespeare Would Text and Drive Too

I spent the afternoon riding the high of being a natural-born dancer. Plus, I felt lucky to have a friend-that's-a-girl who was as much of a romantic as I was. I'd gotten a peek at Valerie's soul that day and supposed she'd taken a gander back at mine.

Still, I felt protective about keeping her in that friend zone. Life was too busy for love as I was now a working professional. I simply couldn't go there. It was about time to clock in for responsibility, theoretically speaking, and literally time to clock in at Chuck E. Cheese. I'd be making $12.50 an hour, so I'd better act like it.

The mysterious damp stench of the costume aside, it felt great to dress up and become someone else for a change. After messing with Tony Rizzio at the tryout, I'd risen above the death threats in my Facebook messages. Hiding behind the face of a giant mouse was a flex.

Damn. I really should have gotten into cosplay.

Too late for that. Time to be an adult and do too

much at once, like my dad. Texting, driving, and eating, all at once. A real professional. I put on a playlist—the best of Fall Out Boy, naturally—and devoured a packet of dry ramen to nourish the evening. Between crunches, I got a video message from Valerie. I glanced up to make sure I wouldn't run somebody over and there I was, dancing. And woah—it wasn't all in my head. I looked pretty dope! She said:

> Look at you in this video! We actually r cute together and you're not a bad dancer, ya big dweeb! If you quit dressing like a sunglass salesman, we make a nice couple!

Immediately after, another text:

> Showed the video to my debate friends. Two of them think you're cute, so when Operation Make Brad Jelly works you might have rebound options waiting for you. I won't say which two tho

I only got 200 texts a month on my phone plan and she was draining it with her fake flirting. It was fake, right? I inched into the slow lane and played along:

> I'll take both so I don't have to decide. Mambo number 5 was right. Polyamory is the future:)

Quick reply:

> Gross, Caldo!!!

I frowned. I wanted to have sex again and soon, but

just as I'd gotten high on my own supply, she couldn't resist bumming me out again. I clapped back:

> You could never be a mormon because ur gross

Valerie:

> You sure about that? Wait til you see me in this! =>.<=

She attached a pic of her prom dress, not her in it. Ugh. It looked like a deep purple envelope with a bedazzled sequin seal in the middle of the chest. And some satin stuff. Roaring twenties? No. It was floor-length. Italian Opera? Victorian? Standard 21st-century prom getup? I didn't know.

> Consult your mom or someone who understands style to figure out how to match. Don't dress like some sloppy lame-o

I wanted to know why her teasing felt endearing. Against my wishes, her salty remarks had started to make me feel warm and cozy. She felt like home. Even looking back at when we first met, she was always like that. She'd agreed to stand by my side and protect me from the hurt of Alexia and the unrelenting taunts of the old people. She did it. Maybe she did it while being a jerk, but she did it. She always showed up when me or other people needed her. I kept a quarter of an eye on the road as I hit back:

> I don't know anything about fashion but Brad is crazy if he sees you in that and doesn't change his mind

The next text was a selfie with Jamie and Michelle. With her reply, my 200-a-month text bank vanished before my eyes:

> Aw CALDO that's sweet I am dead RIP me !!! BTW I decided not to mentor Jamie but be her friend. We have a neurodivergent with the voice of an angel on our hands who needs encouragement and care. She is a baller - I GOT THIS GIRLS BACK && if Fane and that creeper Charles come at her again they will feel my WRATH mwahaha. Also I think Michelle enjoys my company. Don't go in there and treat her like a therapist it's so embarrassing

Valerie really had a way of making people's lives better underneath all that Type A energy was someone with a really kind heart. I said:

> ILYLAS but quit with the novels I'm driving

But lil mama had a lot to say so she came back with an audio file that took forever to load. "Here is our strategy for Operation Make Brad Jelly. We'll get the girls in the limo and swing by to grab you last. I can't wait! But let's get down to business. Now we know you can dance, Caldo, but don't think that's enough. I need you to bring it. Jackie Chan energy. We need to set this up so we're dancing right in front of Brad, but in a way that looks natural and not desperate. Matter of fact, we need the eyes of the entire student body. Get plenty of sleep and pick up some men's vitamins or something. I'm sorry, but this is serious. You need to exude sex appeal and that won't happen overnight without some help. If you don't bring the action, we're fucked! Pardon my French."

She always had to get a neg in there. I opened my own recorder. "Listen, you gotta stop with the negs. I don't care if it's your genius brain coming up with clever little quips. I'm doing my best. You need to relax. Get a medical card or something. We got this. This is our *Silver Linings Playbook* moment. Except you're Bradley Cooper and I'm Jennifer Lawrence. Before you get ideas, I'm not bipolar. I have ADHD, social anxiety, and depression." I laughed. "And you're exacerbating my symptoms. And yes, you should be proud of me. Because this is me setting a boundary! But b-t-dubs, I'm doing all this for you. If that's not love, I don't know what is. I don't know why I said that. Too lazy to re-record. Bye."

Then, a new spiral of questions hit me. Before she could comment, I started another recording. "I probably should have called you at this point so excuse the podcast, and I don't mean to be weird, but if we are dancing and doing the most, doesn't that mean we have to, um, kiss? Siri, send. Siri, send! Is it still recording?"

Minutes of silence. My question made everything feel real.

She opted for a written response:

> Don't worry, we're not going to kiss. But can you act like ur into me? Pretend I have cool crazy hot girl energy, like Alexia - I get it guys like it, that's my whole problem. . . I know I don't have it, but I can pretend to

That made me sad. But I said:

> Nooo, honestly if you weren't so annoying I'd find you cute

She quickly replied:

> LMAO. You finally got a good neg on me. But I really needed to hear that. So thank you :')

Aw. I said the right thing. That felt good. Almost at work, I hit her with one last corny recording. "Thanks for teaching me how to neg like a pro. Beyond Operation Jelly, I'm happy we are doing this. Never would've thought I'd get to go to a dance with a girl in a limo. We've come a long way and I'm really happy I know you. I'm about to switch gears and work for your cousin. But I wanted to say that. I hope you have a good night."

I hit the exit and got a ding back. Her final voice message.

"Since we're being hashtag-honest, and I hope this is alright to say, but I'm kinda hoping Alexia sees our pictures and feels a little jealous, too. I know it's dumb! But I'm also doing this for you. I love our videos and we do look good together. We would actually make sense as a couple. Don't you think? It's funny how we. . . seem to fit. Thank you for doing this, Caldo. It really means a lot. Go be a good mouse, now. I hope you have a good night, too."

Her voice vibrated in my skull. *We would actually make sense as a couple. Don't you think?* It felt like more of a statement than a question, a statement I shouldn't think about too much. I was privy to rumination cycles—wondering what happens when we die, for example. I felt wary of letting it circulate, but as I pulled off the exit, a secret part of me enjoyed riffing on it anyway.

Act 4: Scene 4

The Noble Duties of Rodent Impersonation (Continued)

A collage of kids and pizza and me, chugging Coca-Cola in between hugs and dances until enough hours had passed and my fifteen-minute break arrived. I was tired, too tired to even take the outfit off, so I walked out of Chuck E. Cheese in costume to get some air. The only thing hard about the gig was how damn hot it would get in the mask, and I couldn't take it off unless I was in the small as fuck dressing room.

The change of scene sort of tricked my brain into thinking that it was cooler. But my hair felt alien plastered to my forehead while my ears still rang with the echoes of children screaming my mouse name, their voices distorted through the costume's fuzzy barrier.

I could taste the staleness of recycled air I'd been breathing for hours inside that head, mixed with the tang of my own exhaustion. That mouse head was no joke—fifteen pounds of hard plastic and synthetic fur that sat on my shoulders like a bowling ball, the weight making my neck muscles burn after an hour. The eye holes gave me tunnel vision, turning the world into a fish-eye lens of screaming faces and birthday cake.

And the smell—God, the smell was a cocktail of every previous wearer's panic sweat mixed with disinfectant spray that didn't quite mask the memories of a hundred teenage employees before me. But the strangest part was hearing my own voice bounce around inside that hollow dome, making me sound like I was talking to myself inside an empty bathroom stall. My cheery "Happy Birthday" calls came back to me warped and distorted, a private echo chamber of forced enthusiasm.

I was about to take my mask off and breathe normally when I saw a familiar figure smoking while walking toward me.

Tony fucking Rizzio.

His presence made me sick and scared, as if I was going to shit my pants. He saw me and flicked his cigarette, that awful, sadistic smile spreading across his face.

"What up, Caldo. . . I know it's you. You got that same fearful posture as freshman year."

"What do you want?"

We stood there for a moment, the Florida evening air thick between us.

He took out another cigarette. "I've been going to AA. Step 9 says I gotta make amends and shit. So. . . sorry for being a dick in high school and punching you at iIHOP. My sponsor said when we hurt people, people want to hurt us back. And you already hurt me. Because you hurt my feelings." He sniffled. "So I forgive you, too."

I stared back blankly through my mouse eyes, not convinced this wasn't some setup for more humiliation.

But he continued, "Listen, man. I am in love with her, bro. With Alexia." His voice cracked. "Don't tell no one. And she gets off on my pain like she did with your stupid ass. I know this to be true because she won't text me back. I feel butthurt, a pain I wouldn't even wish on you."

I felt something I never expected to feel for Tony Rizzio: sympathy. "I loved her, too. And it still hurts that she didn't feel the same."

He looked at his feet. "I know, bro. It fucking hurts. You're the only one who gets me."

"You will move on," I said. "It's hard, but I'm doing it. Look at me, I'm at the height of my game. I'm even going to a dance with a girl in a limo."

Tony blew out smoke. "This could be my peak, too. If I can only say yes to life. I met a girl at AA. She was into crystal meth, but young enough so her teeth aren't fucked up. She's got that crystal body, you know."

"That sounds really promising. I'm happy for you."

"We're alright now, you and me?"

I fist-bumped him. "Good luck with the crystal meth girl, and I appreciate you making amends."

"Have fun at the dance," he said and walked pitifully back to his car.

Going back into Chuck E. Cheese I realized that felt like closure. Real closure. Tony would probably always be kind of an asshole, but at least he was trying to be less of one. And somehow, knowing he was hurt by Alexia too made my own pain feel less pathetic.

Maybe we were both figuring out how to be better.

Act 4: Scene 5

Wherein Cupid Striketh, Leaving Orange Kissprints

I felt like a teenage cliché folding my tuxedo neatly and placing it in the backseat before heading to Boca Raton. It was nice to forget about Shakespeare and wander around the Town Center mall. I spent some time in Best Buy fawning over video cameras. It was amazing to see how far technology had come. A reminder I had no excuse not to follow my heart. I was finally facing the future and it didn't feel anxiety-inducing. It was a nice distraction from what would be happening in a few hours. Not sure why it wasn't a real prom date, but it was another rite of passage toward adulthood, and I wanted Valerie to have a good time. Yet there was something icky I couldn't put my finger on, a premonition of us having fun and then Brad swooping in. It all felt like an annoying math problem that I had to live through to figure out what the answer was.

Those hours of strolling around Boca Raton turned into a full day when I left Panera and drove to the retirement home. I wasn't forced by Mom to go to the retirement home today, but there was something about a limo and Valerie coming to my house, with my mother asking a bunch of questions, that felt mortifying. The retirement home felt not only like a lesser of evils but a place where I felt more comfortable being picked up for the only prom I'll probably ever attend.

I made my usual turn off of Glades Road and found a parking space semi-close to the entrance. I grabbed the tux from the back of the car and walked to the entrance with the sun beaming down on me. It felt like a camera doing a close-up and I wondered if my nerves showed through.

I walked into the nursing home holding my tuxedo up like it was a trophy, and Lucy, the usual Guardian of the Welcome Desk, saw me. "Somebody's got a nice tux for tonight. I'm guessing it's not for Alexia, though."

"No, it's for prom. I'm going to have a visitor. Her name is Valerie Diaz. Please buzz her in when she gets here."

Lucy wrote her name down. "Okay. I'll put her down. Also, I am sorry about Alexia. The whole place was rooting for you two, but it looks like you're moving on."

"Yeah, something like that. Valerie is my secret spy prom date."

"Is that some millennial term?"

"No. It means I'm going as her friend."

She buzzed me in. "Well, it's good to have those. Prom can be heaven or hell, going with a friend makes it more likely to be enjoyable."

Heading to the elevator, a crazy ass thought hit me: how would I feel if Valerie and I were going as something more? The idea swirled around while Kenny G.

played, which was supposed to be soothing. Epic failure on its part.

I heard the ding and got off the elevator, carrying the tux carefully on my arm. I really wanted to look good tonight, look my best when we danced together. When I reached my grandma's room I heard an episode of *The O.C.* blasting. I could always recognize Seth Cohen's voice. He sounded a little like me—a better-looking guy but with my same vibe.

There was no answer at Grandma's door. I got concerned and opened the door. "Hey Grandma. Checking in on you. I have my sharp tuxedo from Cousin Michael's Bar Mitzvah, can I put it on in your bath. . ."

My voice came to an abrupt stop as my tux fell to the floor, catching my grandma and Raymond making out in her bed with his hand fully under her blouse.

"Oh shit. . ." escaped my lips.

My grandma removed her orange lipstick lips from Raymond's. For the first time ever, Grandma Goldstein was speechless. Raymond looked indisputably annoyed. He sat up straighter. "Come on, son. Adult things happen in adult living situations. You need to learn to knock."

"I guess you took her to the Cheesecake Factory." It was a nice moment, a feeling of a new family forming. It hit me that I really liked Raymond.

"Go get dressed, I want to take pictures!" my grandma ordered

"And I need a little more of that. Give us a minute."

I took my tux into the bathroom to change. I saw a different person in the mirror than the guy who wore this a year ago at a Bar Mitzvah. I saw a guy who had been through some shit but saw himself more clearly. I didn't see an art film or a virgin or any real label. I saw myself. I saw someone who could take someone like Valerie Diaz to prom.

Act 4: Scene 6

Of Jealousy Performed and Limos Summoned

I posed in my tuxedo—that fit me a little better now while—my grandma took pictures of me with Raymond by her side. In between pictures they snuck kisses while *The O.C.* kept playing on Netflix. It was pretty adorable. It was a little strange to see my grandma with someone. Also her neurotic energy is down by like 50% which makes me wonder if they have had sex, but I don't really want to picture that.

Grandma ran her photoshoot until my cheeks hurt. After what felt like eternity, there was a knock on the door.

"At least someone knows about knocking on doors," Raymond said.

"Come in!" My grandma yelled.

In walked Valerie and holy shit. She looked incredible.

She was wearing a deep purple dress that showed her figure for once, her hair was up in an elegant style, and she was wearing makeup that made her eyes look even more striking than usual— like a completely different person from the frumpy girl who berated me about Shakespeare.

"Wow," I said, forgetting to be cool. "You look. . ."

"Um. Different?" she asked, her eyes hopeful.

"Beautiful." I meant it.

She stared back with an air of disbelief. "You actually look attractive, like really attractive. Huh. Who knew."

"Kids call this kind of flirting negging, Frances. My grandson told me all about it," Raymond said.

"She negged me into being her prom date."

"Valerie, you're beautiful. Maybe even prettier than Alexia, which is impressive. Did you know there are a lot of Latino Jews in the world? It's more common than you think."

"Good to see you, Grandma Goldstein. What do you think, Caldo, am I on Alexia's level in this dress?"

"You know, you might be." Honestly.

"Let me get a pic of you two. Get close. Act like you are going to prom together. Stop being prudes. You're young teens full of hormones, so act like it!" Her voice was raspy. Convicted.

I walked closer to Valerie and she smelled good too. How have I not noticed that Valerie is kind of hot? I put my arm around her shoulder. Our heights were a nice fit, with me being a few inches taller even with her in heels. Chills coursed down my arms. Her shoulders were tight so I could feel the nerves radiating off her. I gently wrapped my hand around them, hoping that doing so would help her feel a little better. We said cheese and my grandma took some pics with her phone. "I'm going to send a few to Alexia. She needs to see what she's missing out on. We are still friends."

"Look at you, Grandma Goldstein, causing trouble.

I dig it," Valerie said. "But alas, we have to go. The chicas are waiting in the limo. It was good to see everyone. And please text those to Caldo. My mom will want them, too."

"Y'all remember this, it's time like these that you are gonna cherish when you're old as hell like us," Raymond said.

"We will," Valerie said and placed her hand on mine. "Lead the way, Caldo."

We walked out with no one watching, holding hands with our bodies becoming more familiar with each other. It felt like I was with a different person, and yet all that time we spent together added up to this moment. I wasn't sure exactly what it was, but it felt good and maybe even right.

We passed through the retirement home lobby while the receptionist cooed, "You two are so cute!"

"I know miracles are real," Valerie agreed, "because we have Joseph Caldo who is maybe even hip." She gave me a sneaky look. "Maybe. Come on. Now, we get to ride in a limo!"

Outside, the limo was even more impressive than I'd expected. The driver, a middle-aged guy in a suit with a radio on his wrist, got out and opened the door for me.

"You must be Caldo. I'm Miguel. The ladies are excited to meet you."

I could hear giggling from inside before I even got in. I stepped behind the wall of tinted windows and was greeted by three girls in beautiful dresses. I took a long, sharp inhale of the scents of hairspray and leather polish. The limo felt like a spaceship, ready to launch into the orbit of these Florida streets.

"Ta-da!" Valerie cheered like I was a fun present to display. The girls giggled.

Instead of feeling like I didn't belong there, I felt like I was where I should be. Reaching into the mini fridge, I cracked open an icy Sprite.

"This is Sam, Tiffany, and Rosa. And ladies, this is Caldo!"

Sam, a tall brunette with intelligent eyes, looked me up and down appraisingly. "So you're the famous Caldo. Valerie's told us so much about you."

"All bad things, I hope."

"Actually," Rosa said, "she said you were funny. She was right."

The girls were sweet. Easy to talk to. Happy to have me there. Asking if guys even noticed when girls flat ironed their hair and wore pantyhose or if they preferred the stripped-down lazy look. I felt like an expert, raising my hands behind my head like a P-I-M-P.

"Valerie says you're a film director?" Tiffany asked.

"I've made my way around the scene."

"That's so cool. I love movies. What's your favorite?"

"Hard to say. I like a lot of different stuff. I glanced at Valerie, hoping she'd chime in, but she watched the road pass by out the window, quietly. Maybe she didn't feel at home at all. "Valerie, you okay?"

She perked up. "Sorry! Yeah. He has a very intellectual taste in films," she said. "Very artistic."

There was something in her tone I couldn't read. Sadness? I changed the subject. "What about you guys? What do you like to do?"

As they talked about their college plans and career goals, I found myself studying Valerie's reflection in the window. When they started debating the merits of different law schools, I saw it as an opportune moment to quietly check in with my friend.

"What's wrong?" I asked.

"Meh." She whistled through a gap tooth, a unique detail I'd never noticed in her face before. "Just worried about seeing Brad."

"Aw. Meh?" I asked. "I'm having lots of fun, but we don't have to do this."

The limo pulled up to the school. Other couples were getting out of cars and limos with their corsages, powdered and sparkled to the nines."

"I'm having fun, too," she said. "I'm sorry. No more meh."

I cocked my head to the side, unconvinced. I grabbed her hand and gave it a squeeze. "Showtime?" I asked.

She covered her mouth. There was the excitement I hoped for. "Showtime."

Act 4: Scene 7

Thy Romance Bloom 'Midst Gymnasium Chaos

The school gymnasium had been transformed with lights and fresh flowers, but it still smelled faintly like floor wax and drips of perspiration.

A DJ in the corner was blasting LMFAO's "Party Rock Anthem" so loud the bass vibrated through the soles of my rented dress shoes and up into my ribcage. Strobe lights sliced the darkness into stop-motion fragments, making everyone's movements look jerky and unnatural. The lights were seizures waiting to happen, but everyone was writhing around anyway, so you couldn't tell the difference. The air was thick with a teenage chemical cloud—Axe body spray battling with Bath & Body Works signature scents in a war that no one could win.

Valerie took my arm as we walked in, and I could feel the tension in her grip. Her fingernails dug tiny half-moons into my forearm through my jacket sleeve. The sequins on her purple dress scratched against my wrist, catching the light in tiny purple-blue explosions with each step we took. Her debate team friends scattered immediately, heading for the punch bowl and leaving us alone.

"There he is," Valerie said quietly, nodding toward the far side of the gym.

I followed her gaze and saw Brad standing with a group of football players and their dates. He was wearing a perfectly fitted tuxedo and looked like he'd stepped out of a magazine. Next to him was a tall blonde girl who stepped out of the same magazine.

"She's pretty," I said, accidentally. "Sorry. I meant to say butt-ugly."

"She's perfect." Valerie was bitter. "Look at her. She probably doesn't even have to try."

I also doubted the girl had to try, but that was irrelevant. The DJ switched to Carly Rae Jepsen's "Call Me Maybe" and the floor erupted in squeals as girls dragged reluctant boyfriends to dance. The temperature in the room seemed to jump ten degrees as bodies packed the dance floor. Someone nearby had clearly snuck in alcohol—the sharp tang of cheap vodka barely disguised by breath mints cut through the sugary smell of the punch table.

"The hell with them, let's hang with your home girls and have some fun," I told her and grabbed her hand.

We found the table with her friends and sat down. The cheap folding chairs were wrapped in white fabric that stuck to the back of my legs through my pants. The tablecloth was tacky beneath my elbows, someone having already spilled punch that no one had bothered to wipe up. That girl Sam immediately scooted her chair closer to mine.

"So, Caldo, want to dance?"

Valerie couldn't keep her eyes off Brad. I needed to

save her. "Maybe later. I promised Valerie the first dance."

"You should dance with Sam. I need to. . . I need a minute," Valerie said.

Before I could protest, she got up and walked toward the bathroom. Sam took my hand.

"She's fiiiine," Sam said. "Let's dance!"

She snatched me up and led me to the floor, my rented shoes sticking to spilled punch with every step. The press of bodies created a wall of heat and the conflicting scents of a hundred different perfumes, colognes, and deodorants failing under pressure. The DJ transitioned to a dubstep remix of some top 40 hit, the bass so heavy I could feel it rattling my teeth. Red and blue lights swept across the crowd, turning everyone's faces into alien landscapes of shadows and highlights.

I let her lead me onto the dance floor, but I kept looking toward the bathroom door. Sam was a good dancer, and she smelled nice, and under normal circumstances I probably would have been thrilled to have a pretty, smart girl paying attention to me.

But all I could think about was the look on Valerie's face.

"You're distracted."

"Sorry. I'm worried about Valerie."

"She's a big girl. She can take care of herself."

"I know, but—"

"But you like her."

"We're just friends."

"Everyone can tell you like her but her. The way you look at her. . . I volunteered to be your rebound, if I'm honest, but I can tell you're not available."

"Sam, you're really great—"

"Story of my life. I always like the guys who are in love with someone else. Maybe one day I can be a homewrecker."

Even if I didn't agree, I appreciated her demented support.

The song ended with a fadeout that seemed to drain all the energy from the room. In the momentary silence before the next track, I could hear the squeak of dress shoes on polished floor, breathless laughter, and the rustle of fancy clothes normally confined to closets. The DJ scratched the next record and a wave of nostalgia hit as "We Are Young" by Fun started playing —that song was impossible to escape that year.

The song ended, and I saw Valerie coming back from the bathroom. She'd fixed her makeup, but she was still shaky.

"Thanks for the dance," I told Sam.

"Anytime. And Caldo? Tell her how you feel. Life's too short to pretend you don't care about someone when you do."

I weaved through the crowd, dodging flailing arms and impromptu dance circles. The air near the edge of the dance floor was cooler, a relief after the tropical heat of packed bodies. A beach ball appeared from nowhere, bouncing from hand to hand above the crowd until a chaperone confiscated it with a constipated-looking eye roll.

I made my way back to Valerie, who was sitting alone at our table, staring at her hands.

"You okay?"

Her eyes were swollen with unshed tears. "He hasn't even looked at me once. It's like I don't exist."

"Maybe that's for the best."

"No, it's not. I need him to see what he lost. I need him to want me back."

"Why?"

The question seemed to surprise her. "What do you mean, why?"

"I mean, why do you need him to want you back? You said it yourself, he's not a good boyfriend. He cheated on you. He doesn't appreciate you."

"Because. . ." she started, then stopped. "Because if he doesn't want me, then maybe I'm not worth wanting."

"Valerie, that's bullshit. You're worth wanting. You're worth so much more than that asshole."

"You really think so?"

"I know so."

The DJ's voice boomed over the speakers, distorted by a microphone that had seen better days. The feedback screeched across the gym, making everyone wince and cover their ears. "Alright everyone, time to slow it down. This one's for all the lovers out there."

The opening notes of "So Tired of Being Alone" by Al Green filled the gymnasium. The music wrapped around us like a warm blanket, somehow creating a bubble of quiet in the chaos. The lights dimmed further, blue and purple hues washing the dancers in a dreamy underwater glow.

I offered her my hand. "Dance with me."

"Caldo—"

"Not for him. For us. Because I want to dance with you."

She looked at my outstretched hand, her fingers fidgeting with the satin edge of her dress. A glitter fleck from someone's makeup had landed on her cheek, catching the light like a tiny star when she finally found my eyes and took my hand.

Act 4: Scene 8

Wherein Feelings Striketh, Brad Blocketh, and Waldo Escapeth

On the dance floor, with Al Green's voice surrounding us and the lights dimmed low, everything else faded away. The world narrowed to just us,—Valerie and me —the gym's chaos receding like a tide pulling back from shore. My pulse synced to the bass line, a rhythm I could feel in my fingertips where they rested against the small of her back. The synthetic fabric of her dress was cool and slippery, with an underlying warmth where it hugged her body. Up close, she smelled like Dove soap and clean laundry, with something uniquely her underneath—a scent I didn't realize existed but now knew I would recognize anywhere.

I could feel her relax in my arms, her body fitting against mine like it belonged there. She smelled like vanilla beans and something floral.

"This is nice," she said quietly.

"Yeah, it is."

The purple and blue lights caught in her eyes, turning them almost iridescent. A strand of her hair had come loose from its careful styling, tickling my wrist as we swayed.

"I'm sorry I've been so weird tonight. I just. . . I don't know what I'm doing anymore."

"That's okay. I don't know what I'm doing either."

"We're quite a pair, aren't we?"

"The best kind."

As Al Green sang about being tired of being alone, I wasn't thinking about Alexia anymore. I wasn't thinking about Brad, or Sam, or anyone else in the gymnasium. I was thinking about Valerie, and how right this felt, and how stupid I'd been not to see it before.

"Valerie?"

"Yeah?"

My mouth had gone dry. I swallowed hard, my pulse thumping in my ears so loud I wondered if she could hear it too. "I'm glad you asked me to be your fake date."

"Me too."

"Even if Brad never notices?"

"Especially if Brad never notices."

The song was building to its climax, strings swelling around Al Green's velvety voice. Someone bumped into us, but we barely noticed, locked in our own gravitational pull. Her eyes dropped to my mouth for a second, but long enough that I noticed. Long enough that I felt brave. I felt myself leaning closer to her. She wasn't pulling away. If anything, she was leaning closer too.

"Caldo?"

"Yeah?"

Her breath was warm against my face, sweet with the cherry punch she'd sipped earlier. The tip of her tongue darted out to wet her lips, leaving them glistening slightly in the dim light. I could feel her fingers tightening on my shoulder, the slight tremble in them traveling through my rented tux jacket.

"This doesn't feel fake anymore."

"No. "My voice went barely above a whisper. "It doesn't." Our faces were inches apart now. I could count her eyelashes, see the tiny constellation of freckles across her nose that even the finest drugstore makeup couldn't hide. The sounds of the gym—the music, the gossip, the woo-hoos—all faded to a distant hum. Life became elastic and endless. This was good film fodder!

Our faces were inches apart now. I could feel her breath on my lips. The whole world had narrowed down to this moment, this girl, this feeling of everything finally clicking into place. And then her lips were on mine, soft and tentative at first, then more certain. Her lip gloss tasted like cinnamon, spicy-sweet. My eyes closed as a current of electricity shot from my lips down my spine, making my knees feel suddenly unreliable. Her hands slid up to my neck, her fingertips cool against my skin, sending goosebumps racing across my shoulders. The world tilted slightly, reality recalibrating around this new certainty: Valerie. Me. Us. This was real. This was—

"Well, well. What do we have here?"

The spell shattered like glass. We broke apart, the cold rush of air between us jarring after the warmth of connection. The music crashed back into my awareness, suddenly too loud. The lights too bright. Reality too harsh. Cringing like two rats before they die in a trap, metaphorical cheese still in our mouths.

Brad was already moving toward us, slow and deliberate, like some oafish security guard who'd spotted kids sneaking into an R-rated movie. He had this stupid smirk on his face, chin tilted up, hands loose at his sides.

"Babe," he said, positioning himself between us with the subtlety of a bouncer. He completely ignored me, his hand sliding onto her waist with territorial confidence. "Mind if I cut in?"

Valerie stepped back, confusion and conflict on her face. Brad stood there like a wall, like he owned her, like I was some security threat he'd neutralized.

"I've been watching you two." His voice got louder, drawing the attention of the crowd around us. "Cute little show. Really convincing."

"It's not a show," I said, puffing my chest as if my inner animal was ready to defend my territory. Fudge muffin! Sam was right.

"Sorry, what was your name again?" Brad gave me an up-and-down and licked his chops, his expression frighteningly amused.

I leaned back. Maybe I wasn't ready to throw down, after all. "Joseph. Caldo."

"Right, Caldo. Like that guy in the striped shirt who hides in pictures."

"That's Waldo," Valerie said, lacking any level of conviction that could possibly make me feel better.

"Same difference." He turned back to her. "Can we talk? Alone?"

I saw her waver. This was the moment she'd been planning for, what this whole night was supposed to be about. But something had changed between us during that dance, and I hoped she felt it too.

"You don't have to talk to him." My voice was only a little peep. The joy had drained from my body.

"She does. We have history. We have feelings. What do you have? A few dance lessons?"

"I have—"

"What? What do you have, Waldo?"

I willed Valerie to say something, to choose me, to tell Brad that what we'd shared meant something. But she stared at the floor.

"I'll be a few minutes," she said, avoiding my gaze.

And like that, she was gone, walking away with Brad toward a corner of the gym where they could talk privately.

I stood there on the dance floor like an idiot while other couples danced around me. Sam appeared at my side.

"I'm sorry. That was rough."

"I should go."

"Or you could stay and show them both that you're not going anywhere."

But I couldn't. I couldn't stand there and watch Valerie choose Brad. I couldn't pretend this didn't hurt. I couldn't be strong and confident when all I felt was small and stupid. I couldn't go through what I went through with Alexia again, and yet she was the only friend I could think of that would be there for me.

I pushed through the crowd toward the exit, hearing Sam calling my name behind me. Whooshing through the door, I pulled out my phone and did something I never thought I'd do. I texted Alexia:

> Need a ride. Prom disaster. At Delray High.

Her response came immediately:

> Good timing. Finally got my license back.

ACT 5

Act 5: Scene 1

Alexia pulled up twenty minutes later in a beat-up Toyota. The day after she got her license back, she's the one rescuing me. I got in without saying anything, and she didn't ask questions. She just started driving.

"IHOP?"

"Yeah."

"Want to talk about it?"

"Not yet."

She turned up the radio. Some sad indie song was playing, which seemed perfect for the moment. We drove through the empty streets of Delray Beach, past strip malls and palm trees and all the familiar landmarks of my disappointing life.

At IHOP, our usual table was empty. The late-night crowd was smaller—a few musical theatre kids balancing spoons on their noses and some glossy-eyed burnouts in rave clothes. Rivera wasn't there, which was probably for the best. I wasn't ready to explain this to anyone yet.

Alexia ordered coffee and pancakes. I got coffee.

"You know it's funny, I knew you'd end up liking her, and it made me jealous, but then relieved. So," she said after the waitress left. "What the hell happened? I saw the cute photos from your grandma, you do make a nice couple, which is a little soon and hurts my ego, but I get it."

I told her everything. The dancing, the kiss, Brad showing up, and Valerie leaving with him. By the time I finished, my coffee was cold and Alexia was looking at me with sympathy and frustration in equal measure.

"You left." It wasn't a question.

"I left."

"Without fighting for her."

"What was I supposed to do? She made her choice."

Alexia rubbed her temples like she needed an Alka-Seltzer. "Can I be brutally honest with you?"

"Do I have a choice?"

"You acted like a pussy. You go from one extreme to another instead of letting things happen in their own time. You did that with me, and you did the other extreme with her."

"It's different. She walked away with him, Alexia. After we kissed. After she said it felt real, she went with him."

"She walked away to talk to him. That's not the same thing as choosing him."

"What's the difference?"

"The difference is that if you'd stayed, you would have been there when she came back. You would have been able to tell her how you felt instead of running away like a scared kid."

Her words stung because they were true. "I was

scared. I don't know. What happened with us it fucking sucked, and I didn't want to feel it again."

"I know. But Caldo, you can't keep letting fear make your decisions for you. What if she was talking to Brad to say it was over? What if she was coming back to choose you?"

"What if she wasn't?"

"Then at least you would have known. As of now, you can't be sure so it makes sense for you to feel regret."

I stared into my coffee, feeling the weight of my own cowardice. "I keep fucking all this stuff up."

"No. You aren't, you're a high school guy, which makes you dumb by default. But it's not too late to fix it."

"She's probably back with him now."

"You don't know that! She might be sitting in her room, wondering where the hell you went and why you didn't fight for her." Alexia, of all people, was ready and willing to help clean up my mess just as we'd done with the banana pudding.

"What should I do?"

"What do you want to do?"

"I want to tell her I'm falling for her. I want to tell her that kiss meant everything to me. I want to tell her that Brad's an idiot if he doesn't see how amazing she is."

Alexia smiled. "So tell her."

"What if she doesn't feel the same way?"

Alexia reached across the table and took my hand. "Then at least you'll know you tried. And Caldo? You're a good guy, you have to have your actions match and be stronger. But honestly, with you and Valerie, I saw something real with you two together. Opposites attract, and you two are definitely opposites. At the same time, you're similar in all the right ways. She'd be lucky to have a guy like you. Stop acting like you're not good enough. It's not true, and it's not attractive. You are better than that."

Act 5: Scene 2

Of Stars and Second Chances

Outside IHOP, the Florida night was clear and warm. Alexia lit a cigarette and looked up at the sky.

"You can see the stars tonight."

I followed her eyes up. She was right—for once, the light pollution wasn't too bad, and you could see stars scattered across the dark sky.

"Make a wish," she said.

"That's shooting stars."

"Any stars. Come on, humor me."

I tried to make a pattern out of the scattered points of light. I knew instantly what I wanted the most. It wasn't hard.

"What did you wish for?" she asked.

"Can't tell you. It won't come true."

"That's superstitious bullshit."

"I'm not taking any chances."

She guessed my wish anyway and said, "I hope you get her, too."

We stood there for a few more peaceful minutes.

For the first time in weeks, I wasn't anxious about anything. I was present, at that moment, with my dear friend.

She crushed her cigarette underneath her heel. "I'll get you home."

In the car, she put on a mix of emotional house music—the type I imagined college kids cried to at the club when they felt nostalgic—and we cruised through the empty streets.

When we got to my house, she turned to me.

"Caldo. I'm proud of you. You've come so far from the scared kid who used to visit his grandma to avoid dealing with life."

"Thanks. For the memory of us. Having fun. For all of it."

We car-hugged, fumbling over enormous, empty Big Gulp cups, then I got out and watched her drive away.

I stood in my driveway for a few more minutes, afraid to spend time alone with myself, but doing it anyway. This was processing. Inside, the house was dark. My parents had left a note saying they'd gone to bed early and that there was leftover Chinese food in the fridge if I was hungry. I wasn't.

I went upstairs and sat on my bed, still in my wrinkled tuxedo, staring at my phone. I could text Valerie. I could call her. I could drive to her house and throw pebbles at her window like some romantic comedy hero.

But I was still scared. Still convinced that she'd chosen Brad, that I'd imagined the connection between us, that I was setting myself up for another low blow.

I fell asleep with my phone in my hand, my tuxedo

wrinkled beyond repair, and my wish still hanging in the air like a prayer I wasn't sure anyone was listening to.

Act 5: Scene 3

The Shrink Sayeth "No Shit, Sherlock"

I woke up disoriented, still in my tuxedo pants and dress shirt, my phone dead on the pillow next to me. I wanted to go back in time. I felt true regret, wishing that I could have stayed, and nothing reminded me more of that regret than seeing not even one text from Valerie. Did I lose her? Would she have told Brad she found someone new and that person was me?

This feeling was so similar to when my mom took my camera away and I wished I could go back in time and not follow that old man. Emptiness and regret, which no one under twenty-one should probably ever feel, flooded my mind and body. Valerie and I were both high school romantics, opposites and yet something happened that night. Something magical and I killed it by being a coward.

I stared at my phone wondering if I should call her but I had to do this in person and I needed to know what the fuck was wrong with me. I called Dr. Heller, knowing that this wasn't really an emergency, but it felt like one.

"Hello, this is Dr. Heller. Joseph, are you okay?"

"Nah, man. I'm not. I'm not suicidal or any of that, but I'm not okay I'm and just, like, wondering, why are we doing this? Like, what is this really doing for me?"

"Ah, okay. But you're okay physically? Not going to harm yourself?"

"Come on! You know I don't like pain! But anyway, how do I push through this and live? I've been living like a ghost, haunting the halls of my own life. I'm the creaking sound in my own metaphorical floorboards. I need to free myself. It's time to get it together."

"Can you be a little more specific, Joseph? I was about to microwave my Amy's Tofu Scramble."

"I'll be quick. Alexia and I are friends again. When I kissed the mentor girl Valerie I realized I was over all that. I realized I'd become a fool for Valerie by being her fake prom date. I feel like a complete sap! And now we still have to do a Shakespeare performance even after what happened at prom. And I'm supposed to—what—pretend I don't feel this way?"

"That's a lot of quick changes, but there is no need to panic. This is how it goes right before adulthood. Does Valerie feel the same?"

"I think she might, but her ex looks like Tim Tebow! I panicked and ran. What chance do I have?"

"Joseph, I say this with compassion. You screwed up. You need to tell the girl right away how you feel. There are no pills or things I can do to get you to do that, so I am going to go and let you finally embrace your life from the dead, or however you put it. Goodbye and good luck."

I hung up from Heller with a charge of inspiration to run to school and convince Valerie that a male Amélie was better than a poor man's Tebow. But instead, I saw a text message waiting for me from Raymond. I opened it and found a jarring 911:

> Hey son, it's an emergency. I need you to come and see me now. You gotta come, your grandma needs you. I'll tell u more when you get here. Come now!

Act 5: Scene 4

I drove to the retirement home a wreck, worried about Grandma and worried about what the hell to say to Valerie or even do for this project. She probably thought I skipped school, afraid to face her, an even bigger coward than I'd been at the dance. Maybe I would have done that anyway, but more importantly, I needed my grandma and Raymond to be alright.

I wasn't so much afraid for their health as I was that they'd broken up and were causing some scorched-earth commotion. Love is hard no matter what the age. Couldn't they endure it? For the love of God? They were my only hope after I'd botched my central plotline.

I pulled in and turned off the engine, but I wasn't able to move. I felt stuck, like I was carrying all the weight of my entire life, yet I couldn't let go. Dr. Heller told me one time he had a private catharsis when he screamed at himself alone in his car. *No one there to judge you*, he'd said. *Just let it all out*.

I howled from my gut, slamming my hands onto the

rearview mirror and yanking it toward my face. My stupid red nose scorched like barbecued kishke. "C'mon, man. You fucking piece of shit! All you needed was faith in yourself! You couldn't even give yourself that!" I pointed at myself, ready to smash the glass of my reflection. I wagged my finger. "You pathetic little—"

Someone was hysterically laughing outside my window. Oh my god. Peering out the corner of my eye, I saw a camera pointing right in my face. Damnit! Why did cameras keep catching me at my worst moments? I'd been cursed as punishment for putting my true passion to the side. Are you there, God? It's me, Caldo, praying no one would post it on Facebook.

It was Raymond's grandson. "What up y'all! Look at this dude. What up, man? You got some serious serial killer vibes. Screaming at yourself outside of an old folks' home. Oh. Wait a sec, sir. Do you have Benjamin Button disease? My bad. What are you, like seventy?"

"I don't have Benjamin Button disease. I'm seventeen."

"What the hell are you doing at an old folks' home, then, man? Do you spank it to GILFs? Ain't no shame!"

"No."

"Ah, come on. Don't lie to the cam. No one lies to my cam. That's why they follow me. Black Logan Paul makes sure everyone keeps it real. What's your deal, my dude?"

"Man, I really don't want to be on camera right now. I'm here cause your grandfather called me. He said it was an emergency."

Jamal turned his camera off. "Shit, for real? Is something wrong? He just said I needed to get here and bring my camera." He held it up proudly, showing it off.

I got out of the car. "Sony NEX-FS700. That's a nice camera."

"Only the best. You know your shit, but how do you know Pop Pop?"

"I kind of hooked him up with my grandma."

"What? Ah man, I told Gramps not to mess with white girls."

"I'm sorry, okay? But they love each other. If it's any consolation, South Florida Jews are pretty woke. Plus, have you seen *I'm Through with White Girls*? He ends up with an African-American Canadian with cool dreads, it is a real and fraught examination of true love."

"How the hell do you know that movie? White kids aren't supposed to watch that movie. That's the whole point."

"Listen. I know my way around. I've seen it all."

"Have you? Cause I saw you losing your goddamn mind by yourself in broad daylight."

"You're catching me on an off day," I said defensively. "Anyway, I like your setup. I wish I was making a film, too, instead of rotting on the couch and watching DVDs."

"You're a weird dude, man. Film something, then. Feels like a non-issue."

Grandma appeared and cut us off. She and Raymond had entered, holding hands, but she broke free and plowed toward me like she was about to grab my ear. "Joseph! What are you doing here? You should be in school!"

Raymond chuckled. "Check it out, Franny. Our grandsons linked up. Jamal, start that camera up. Get a shot of us all together cheesing."

"Joseph, explain yourself. Raymond, did you plan this? Why are you having me go outside? What time is it? We are going to miss pickleball! Nice to meet you, Jamal! But please put that camera down. I haven't powdered my forehead. But whew. It's too hot out here. Are we supposed to play on the outside courts today? They're baking us like yams. Joseph, you forgot to bring me batteries for my face fan."

"Never mind the fan, Franny. I got double-A's inside. Don't stop shooting, Jamal. I ain't got much of my life left before I cash in my chips."

Then, he held his back and lowered to the ground, one knee down on the concrete. He let out a painful sigh, somehow still in the tune of joy.

"Oh shit," Black Logan Paul and I said in unison.

A little tear rolled down Grandma's cheek. We all smiled, except for Jamal who stared in shock, his arm barely holding the camera up, the lens aimed toward the ground. Was he insane? He was clouded by shock, incapable of doing the moment justice. He didn't deserve that camera. He was killing the mood.

I tapped on his shoulder gently. "Can I have this, please? I'll get the video."

Jamal stood dumbfounded. Unresponsive. I took it gently out of his frozen hands. The sleek, cool texture felt right at home in my palms. It had been seven years since I'd held one, but I re-engaged from muscle memory—an extension of me. For the first time since the accident, I felt like myself again. The curious young Caldo, not yet tarnished by tragedy. The one who still loved himself, the one who had hope.

I zoomed into Raymond's face and panned slowly to Grandma's, savoring the sparkling, surreal moment.

"Frances," he said, his voice carrying across the parking lot. "Will you do me the honor of being my wife?" Through the viewfinder, I saw the world more clearly—my grandmother's face lighting up like a sparkler, Raymond's tremoring hand as he pulled out the ring. Even the Floridian heat came through, melting across the screen like butterscotch over a sundae.

"Yes!" she squealed. "Yes, you beautiful man. Yes!"

I kept the camera on them as they kissed and moved to a shot of the ring sliding onto her finger. Perfect. Not a tremor in sight.

A gaggle of nosey residents wandered outside to join the commotion. Ooo-ing and ahh-ing as they congratulated them. Some wondered aloud if they'd ever find love again. Others started complaining about how their late spouses didn't give them the royal treatment and thanked heaven they were dead. Others wept into handkerchiefs, savoring the memories. So much good B-roll. So many sound bites.

Grandma showed off her ring to anyone who would look. A diamond nestled between two pieces of coral, unfiltered and real. She turned to me and flashed a grin like a schoolgirl on picture day. The orange of her ring matched her lipstick, adding that extra pop.

For a moment, I saw her as Frances—not Grandma. She beamed before me as if she was in a slideshow of her every age. From her first laugh to her own school dances, caught with a Kodak and sent to the stop baths in the dark rooms of Eckard's. Frances. A sweet and sour clementine. And I got to capture it. She wanted me to be proud of her, our dynamic for a moment in reverse. I was proud of her. So proud. Love had come knocking by surprise and she said yes. The finest moment of my young life. All was right and good with Frances, which reminded me of the other things I needed to make right, too. Valerie.

When love came to me, I'd drawn the blinds like a fool.

"Jamal, can I borrow this for a few hours? We're in-laws now. I really need it today to make things right in my life."

He gave me a once-over, making sure he liked me before deciding we were family.

"Godspeed," he said. "The magic is in your hands."

Act 5: Scene 5

Wherein Our Hero Claims His Destiny

Everyone—I mean everyone—was congregated on the playground by the time I arrived. A flustered Valerie was talking to Miss Connie while the kids were playing, with Fane and Charles watching with amusement. Even Jamie was there, sitting with Michelle near the monkey bars. Valerie was slumped over, defeated.

Ah shit. She was probably telling Connie the mentorship was done because she couldn't stand working with me. The director in me could tell what was happening without even hearing a word and everyone was loving the drama. Even the kids knew that a battle was happening between Connie and Valerie that rivaled The Avengers vs Loki. That protective feeling took over the energy I felt before I turned into the Cowardly Lion at prom. Making her laugh, even at my own expense, always felt worth it. Forget Bar Mitzvahs. Self-recognition is what turned boys into men.

I looked in the back seat at Jamal's camera. I needed it, I needed it to be my best self to make things right and fix what might not even be fixable. I took one of those deep breaths a choir teacher begs kids to take mid-song so they don't botch the final high note at the school assembly. I exhaled, grabbing the camera and walking out of the car to the playground to overhear Valerie say, "I've never failed at anything, but I think this might be the time it happens. I can't mentor him. I can't do this project. . ." Her eyes caught mine and her voice came to a halt.

All the playground eyes turned to me holding up the camera, "I am not letting either of us fail. I failed you miserably last night, and I won't do that again."

"Caldo," Valerie said, and until that moment, I had never heard five different conflicting emotions in someone saying my name. But her thought ended there. For the first time ever, she was speechless. My cowardice didn't just hurt me. I really hurt her. I rejected both of us last night.

"Could we talk somewhere else? Please."

"No, your chance to talk to me in private was last night and you lost that chance. You can say whatever you want right here. I feel so done with everything."

"That's fair. I'll do it here and now, then," I said. I turned on the camera and placed it on a slide pointing toward the merry-go-round, which looked a little like a stage. It seemed like the perfect ambiance for what I had to say and I stepped on top of it. It spun a tiny bit and I said, "Miss Connie, let this be part of our project, the meta aspect of how Shakespeare can reflect the lives of high schoolers even now, in the present day. Now, we will find out if the hero can surpass his follies and find his way back to Valerie's heart." I paused. "I'm the hero. In case that wasn't clear."

"Interesting. Didn't see that coming. Okay. You

have the stage, Your project is officially being graded now."

"Shakespeare basically says you can't escape what you feel whether it's attraction, ambition, or resentment. We are at the behest of our feelings and sometimes can't escape them. When looking at these plays, we see the real tragedy is ourselves and how we feel. We aren't robots. We have hearts that get broken, usually by our own doing. But how we react to these feelings is whether we have a tragic life or one of joy and comedy. In each of Shakespeare's plays, this is what defines the genre—whatever the hero decides is his fate."

"Wow. That's astute."

"Thank you." I continued, "My tragedy is I got lost in a surge of angst and hormones. I fell in love with the first girl that caught my eye even though I knew deep down it wouldn't work. Then, I met someone who made more sense—our fair Valentina here—and I blew it. I'd been scorned by my first love so when these feelings came up again, I ran off like the biggest puss. A pussalinious fool. I learned that word in a SAT class I dropped."

"I think you mean pussy," Jamie said. "Sorry. This is better than *Gossip Girl.*"

"Shush!" Connie said. "I'm trying to hear."

Valerie finally walked forward and stepped on the merry-go-round with me. "I wish you had stayed," she said. "You hurt my feelings. You made me feel like I wasn't worth standing up for. Why couldn't you wait and be patient with me? All I needed was closure with Brad before I made a decision. Instead, you made it for me. How can I be with a guy who doesn't think he's good for me? If a guy doesn't believe he's good enough, then why should a girl be expected to root for him? Shakespeare taught us that romantic love, passion, and connection are always worth the fight, even if these things lead to tragedy. It's been there all along. You didn't do the assignment."

"I *did* do it," I said. "The real one. But somehow I missed the secret one, the one between us. I wasn't sure you felt the same."

"Why not take the risk anyway? Why not even ask?"

"Because even the question is scary sometimes."

"Caldo, it's like Shakespeare said: Cupid is a knavish lad, thus to make poor females mad. You already know you make me crazy. Of course I feel the same."

"I make you crazy?"

"See? You think I'm all buttoned up, like everyone else. Like I can't handle things. Like I have no darkness. I'm a teenage girl, too. Maybe I've never snuck out my bedroom window in the night or gotten my bellybutton pierced or even ever smoked a Swisher Sweet, but you can't assume I don't have something else inside. Something that wants things, something that likes to show off and get told I'm hot. Something that sometimes makes me feel a little stupid or a little guilty. Everyone expects too much from me. That girl is in here, too. The one that's rebellious. The one with a secret I only show a careful selection of people through long eye contact. The one I shared with you. I'm sorry I've never had my license revoked. Maybe every Ivy League institution in America is begging for me to enroll with them, but I'm still this girl," she said. She lifted up the bottom of her dress and showed me an anklet, one of those gold chains they wear in the hip hop videos that said 'Val' in a cursive.

"Holy fuck," I blurted. "Sorry. Go on."

"I'm a 21st-century American girl. I want to ride off into the night on a motorcycle with some guy."

"I'm not that guy. But I can be that guy. . . metaphorically. If you'll let me."

"Then why didn't you? You left me behind and went to meet someone you think is more interesting."

"That's not it. That's not why I ran. I ran because I was scared. I ran because I tend to ruin things for myself. I ran because I don't think I deserve nice things. But you're more than a nice thing. Clearly." I gestured to her ankle. "But besides that badass ankle bracelet thingy, I did pick up on your dark side, and I did see the eye contact. I see you. You *are* interesting. That's what's scary."

She lowered her dress again and tried to hide a grin, but the cute little gap tooth I'd just discovered shone through anyway.

I swooped my hair and pulled a toothpick out of my pocket. This was the monologue moment. The one where I professed my life. "Listen. We're the same. Everyone thinks I'm buttoned up, too. For different reasons. I don't know where my self-deprecation comes from, but I'm working on it every day. If you think I have any confidence, you're wrong. Not that it's your job to give me confidence. You have enough jobs. But, if you'll let me, I want to take some of that off my plate. My biggest regret in life has been not taking risks. Holding myself back. Little details get me down, from giving up on my cinematography passion entirely, all the way to leaving you behind at the dance. Fear has ruined my life. Then I met you. Someone who felt out of reach and above me. All this time, I've felt like a loser, not like the motorcycle muscle guy. I think you are magical," Then, I felt it. Real love. The sort of love that's founded on friendship but decides to be committed, decides to be intimate. I always wanted a girlfriend. I wanted her to be it. I pulled the toothpick out of my mouth and threw it off the side of the merry-go-round. "Valerie. Will you do me the honor? Can we give this a chance?"

She shifted back and forth, looking around at what felt like everything but me. The world whirred on. Finally, we caught eyes. "If you're wondering what's in it for you," I said, "It's a boyfriend who will love you." She ran her fingers through her hair. A small dimple appeared in her cheek.

"Maybe you can have a girlfriend who will love you, too."

"Straight women have no standards these days!" Fane cried. "That's the damn truth!" Charles echoed.

"Quiet, everyone!" Connie yelled. "This is. . . art. . . I think. Carry on."

"Miss Connie is right. Art is what matters. Art helps us understand that life makes no sense, but it's beautiful to try to understand it. From Shakespeare to the pop songs on Kiss FM, we're all trying to understand it. To understand love. I wanted to be an Avenger, but you're right. I'm Amélie. A male Amélie. I should have known what you wanted all along."

"Caldo, enough. You talk too much. Shut up and come here." She inched a little closer to me.

Then, she kissed me—as the merry-go-round went round—which was met with resounding claps and cheers. Valerie and me, a crowd-pleasing arthouse sensation. Of all the times throughout human history a girl told a guy to shut up, this time was the most beautiful. Jamie cried and sang the *Titanic* song. Eyes of onlookers welled with emotion—a memory made before them that no one would forget. Whether we were stars in a Shakespearean adaptation or just two kids in some shaky homemade video, we got the happy ending we needed by creating something new we both wanted.

About the Authors

Christoph Paul is the EIC of CLASH Books and an award-winning humor and horror author. He was the Singer/Songwriter of The Dionysus Effect, and the forthcoming Goth rock band Doriana Gray & electro Goth project The Sheep Look Up. He has a flip horror book with two novellas *The Last House on Earth & Death Walks South Boston*, and the chaos magick horror novel *Cosplay to Death* forthcoming with Shortwave Publishing.

Caroline Macon Fleischer is an author and theatre artist. Her books include the literary horror *A Play About A Curse* (October 2025) and the psychological thriller *The Roommate* (2022). She teaches English at Loyola University and writes with the typewriter poetry collective, Poems While You Wait. She lives in Chicago with her husband and son. See more @caromacon and www.caromacon.com

Both Christoph and Caroline also want to say how much they loved working with Angela Capovani who was an amazing editor for this book.

ALSO BY CLASH BOOKS

HORROR FILM POEMS

Christoph Paul

A PLAY ABOUT A CURSE

Caroline Macon Fleischer

ALL OUR TOMORROWS

Amy DeBellis

AEMRICAN THIGHS

Elizabeth Ellen

GAG REFLEX

Elle Nash

MULHOLLAND DIVE

Vanessa Roveto

LOVER GIRL

Nicole Sellew

I CAN FIX HER

Rae Wilde

GIVE ME DANGER

Tea Hačić-Vlahović

THE STYLE OF YOUR LIFE

Brittany Ackerman

www.ingramcontent.com/pod-product-compliance
Lightning Source LLC
Chambersburg PA
CBHW030134010826
48973CB00002B/562

9781960988652